THE FASTEST FRIEND
IN THE WEST

Other books by
VICKI GROVE:

Junglerama
Goodbye, My Wishing Star

THE FASTEST FRIEND IN THE WEST

Vicki Grove

AN
APPLE
PAPERBACK

SCHOLASTIC INC.
New York Toronto London Auckland Sydney

ISBN 0-590-44338-0

12 11 10 9 8 7 6 5 4 3 2 1   2 3 4 5 6 7/9

Printed in the U.S.A.   28

First Scholastic printing, February 1992

To KATHY
with love and gratitude

Contents

PART 1 ★ Lorelei Among the Land Creatures   9

PART 2 ★ Vern's Story   95

PART 3 ★ Back at Sea Level   163

Chapter 1

～**W**hen we moved into our locker the third day of seventh grade, about the first thing Louise did was to stick this gross mirror onto the back wall.

"Come and look, Lor!" she said, as she was adjusting the little magnetic strips that held it on. "You can see your whole hair at once and everything!"

What choice did I have? I stepped close beside her, and saw my pudgy face with its frame of dark, wiry hair grimacing back at me from beside her slim, beautiful, golden-haired reflection.

Over the next six weeks I learned to yank the locker door open, hard. A little over half the time, that would send the mirror skidding to knee level.

But on October 17, the day she moved out, I wasn't that lucky. Dr. Foster had drilled my molar that morning, and I returned to school after fifth period, my left jaw numb and my stomach growling from no lunch. I jerked extra hard on the locker door, but the dumb mirror held tight. So the first thing I saw inside our locker was my face wearing a Novocain-stiff, peeved expression.

The second thing I saw was that Louise's junk (except for the mirror, of course) was gone.

And the third thing I saw was the note. It was attached to the inside of the door with one of those Band-Aids Louise kept in her purse for the blister on her left heel.

"Hi, Lor," it read. "Don't be mad, okay?"

I wasn't mad, exactly. It was more like the rest of me just suddenly got as numb as my jaw. I knew in a sickening flash she'd moved in with Cheryl Hopkins, to be in the section of the hall where the popular girls have their lockers.

I was too afraid to chance seeing myself again in the mirror right at that moment, so I couldn't rummage in the half-empty locker for the notebook I needed for study hall. Besides, I really couldn't face sticking around, hoping I ran into Louise, and hoping I didn't. I slammed the locker door. As it clunked shut, I heard the mirror slide to the floor.

Then I ran out of the school. I wanted to keep running, but when I reached the sidewalk I was afraid I'd slip and fall. Tears were blurring my vision, and the concrete was slick and gross with wet leaves. They were giving up on the dead trees, dropping all over the place in pathetic, soggy glumps.

I knew exactly how they felt.

*   *   *

When I reached the house Mom turned out to be home already from Sunshine Day Care Center, where she works part-time as a cook. I hated to have to answer a bunch of questions, but she was in the kitchen cooking something that smelled delicious, and I didn't think I could stand another minute of this awful day on an empty stomach.

"Hi, Sweetcakes," she said, shooting me a worried combination smile-frown when I came in and sat on a barstool. "What's cookin'?"

Mom sometimes talks foodtalk, like some little kids talk babytalk. You've got to get used to it.

"Nothing. My tooth just hurts and I'm only missing phys. ed. and study hall," I muttered, sticking a finger into the butterscotch sauce she was stirring. Then, without thinking, I asked her a question. "Mom, were you already fat when you were a kid?"

She turned quickly back around from the stove, her tent dress sailing and shifting around her like—well, like a tent.

"Already?" she asked, pink exploding up her neck.

"Not that you're fat now," I said quickly. "But that metabolism thing you're always saying you and I have that keeps us from being skinny and athletic like Daddy. When you were a kid, did you ever try to, you know, get rid of it?"

She laughed then, and when she reached across the counter to pat my hand the loose skin under her arm flapped around. I felt my own arm, trying to make it look like I was scratching a bug bite. No flab, exactly. More like just a lot of flesh.

"Lori Lynn, now don't you go worrying about your metabolism. You have a face pretty as a peach in August, and beautiful eyes. Have some cake to make you feel better."

I took the cake, and wandered down the hall toward my room, thinking about eyes. They just don't really count much. Most of the popular girls, Cheryl Hopkins included, have run-of-the-mill eyes. But you see their hair and figures first, and by then you're too dazzled to even notice whether they have eyes or not.

And when you stop to think about it, what could be more disgusting than having a big, round peach face?

★ ★ ★

In my room, the comforting sounds of my aquarium filters greeted me, as they have every day since I got my fish for my eighth birthday. I flopped down on my bed, carefully balanced the plate of cake on my stomach, and tried to let the awful day be carried off to sea.

I looked to my side, to the big mirror my fifty-gallon aquarium makes. There, I always look altogether different than in Louise's gross locker mirror, or than in my own vanity mirror. I look wistful and thin, my hair flowing in a melancholy rush till it seems to tangle with the seaweed in the tank. I seem a mermaid. In fact, there's actually very little to keep me from thinking I am inside that tank instead of merely reflected back from the outside. Inside with my fish— my friends.

My only real friends now, I thought, since Louise moved out on me.

That thought was so depressing I had to close my eyes tight to keep new tears from leaking into my hair.

It was a little hard to eat my cake, with my eyes squeezed shut like that.

Chapter 2

Some small, stupid part of me kept thinking Louise might come to her senses and realize that she couldn't live without my friendship. So my palms were sweating hopefully the next morning as I walked into school and peered into the gym where everybody has to wait until the first-hour bell rings at 8:15.

I stared across the packed bleachers toward "our" place, the seat Louise saved for me all through sixth grade and the first forty-seven days of seventh. There's a little roof over that seat because the second tier of bleachers juts out like an umbrella above it, so it's the only place in the entire gym where you're not out in the open so everybody can gawk at you. Louise was shy like me back in sixth grade when she picked that place.

She wasn't there, of course.

I really dreaded having to cross the gym to sit in that spot alone, but somehow I made it. When I got there I pretended to study my history. Then I pretended to read the banners on the gym wall. They aren't that interesting, but you have to do something to prove you're a normal person when nobody's sitting with you. Lady Basketball Bluebirds, District Champions '84, '85, '87, '88. Volleyball Bluebirds, Conference Champs '84, '87. They go on like that—we've got good teams at Greenpoint Middle School.

When the 8:15 bell rang, I made the awful mistake of glancing up toward the top row of bleachers, where the popular girls cluster together like a bunch of bright fruit. Louise was up there, laughing. She caught my eyes, and her neck turned red.

I made a vow not to ever, ever look up there again.

★   ★   ★

I had so much on my mind that morning that I left my purse in the gym and had to go back in to look for it after school.

I'd never been in the gym when it was empty and quiet like that before. It seemed like a church or something, so big and lit only with weak autumn sun dribbling through the skylights. I had always hated the gym, since it was the location of the two truly gruesome parts of school—phys. ed., and waiting for the 8:15 bell to ring. But it looked peaceful and almost beautiful that afternoon, with the light dim and mellow and mysterious like in a huge aquarium.

There was a ball lying loose over by the bleachers, and before I knew what I was doing, I put down my books and walked over to pick it up.

It had crossed my mind a couple of times in the past twenty-four hours that maybe if I was outstand-

14

ing at some sport or something Louise would like me again. Maybe I was meant to be outstanding at something, and I just hadn't hit on what yet. Maybe I had some great natural talent that I would stumble on when I least expected it, and since I expected it less all the time that meant the time of discovery could be quite near.

I sometimes do contests with myself to determine directions for my life, and that's what I did then.

"I, Lori Sumner, have never sunk a basket in my life," I chanted solemnly. "If I sink this one, I shall become committed to the game of basketball."

I realized with a quick little ache that those were the first words I'd said at school all day, except for "Gettysburg," in answer to a question Mr. Parkins had asked me in history.

I bent at the knees, sprung up, and released the ball into the shadowy gym air. It missed the backboard by maybe three feet, maybe four.

"Oh no, I can't believe it! Ha!" Hysterical laughter exploded behind me, laughter coming from the back of the dimly lit gym. I whirled around to see five of the popular girls lounging on the tumbling mats, probably taking a break from cheerleading practice. They'd been watching me the whole time! Louise jumped up from among them and came quickly toward me.

"Don't mind them, Lor," she said in a whispered rush. "Listen, I was going to explain yesterday before I moved my stuff, but you were, you know, gone. It's just that, well, you and I don't have much in common anymore, you know?"

"Did you guys hear what I said?" I croaked out. "About becoming committed to basketball?"

But I knew the answer to that. Over Louise's shoulder I saw Cheryl Hopkins and Julie Andersen still collapsed in giggles, their faces mostly hidden behind the glowing sheets of their long hair.

"You could have warned me, Louise," I mumbled. "You could have let me know you guys were watching."

"Sorry, Lor," she said, looking like she truly was. "I mean, I'm sorry about everything, okay?"

Her hair was as shimmery and perfect as Cheryl's now. Toward the end of spring last year her mother took her to a doctor for her complexion, and the doctor made her lose seventeen pounds and start washing her hair every night.

That, in a nutshell, was what she meant we didn't have in common anymore.

"Are you okay?" she repeated.

"Yeah, sure," I said. What else could I say? I turned, got my books, grabbed my purse, and somehow made it out of the gym.

Chapter 3

Except for dinner, I spent that afternoon and night in my room, sitting on the floor watching my giant angel fish, Louise (needless to say, I named her back in sixth grade). She kept trying to eat the tails of the orange platys. I'd never noticed that ruthless streak in her before.

"Knock, knock. Private party in there, or can anybody crash? Gotta have fins, or will my old snorkel and mask do?"

I rolled my eyes, then got up and hurried to open the door.

"Oh, Daddy," I said, glad he'd come to check on me.

He stood there, his eyes all big and worried behind his glasses, his hands deep in his pockets. His grayish brown frizzy hair was sticking up in all directions, and the red pencil he uses to grade papers with was sticking out over his left ear.

"You didn't have much to say at dinner, Lori-dori. Or last night, either. Catfish got your tongue?"

I keep thinking I'll quit laughing at Daddy's corny fish jokes, but I always forget when the time comes. This time, though, my laugh kind of turned to a sob. He opened his arms, and I felt tears leaking out onto his T-shirt as I hugged him.

"Boy, seventh grade. The pits sometimes, huh?"

"Yeah," I whispered. He knows, too, because he used to teach it before he switched to teaching senior high.

"Still, any pit usually has a high point somewhere close beside it. I mean, they've got to put all that stuff they dig out of the pits somewhere, right? So they make it into mountains."

He can't help the weird way he sometimes sees the world. He teaches science. And it wasn't that I couldn't get the point he was trying to make, but teachers and fathers have the job of trying to make the whole world sunny for people. All I'd thought about for the past two miserable days was the coming months, and I was pretty sure I had a more realistic outlook than Daddy did. I sure couldn't see any high point to a year spent sitting alone and gawked at in the gym, and being the only seventh grader who didn't have a locker mate.

So I didn't answer. After a while he cleared his throat, still patting my back.

"Lori-dori Mermaid, living in the sea-shade, diving 'neath the coral glade, Lori-dori Mermaid," he sang, off-key.

That dumb rhyme of his always cheered me up

when I was about eight. I didn't want to hurt his feelings, but it was about four years too late for it to do that now.

Still, it felt good having him just hold me like that.

* * *

When Daddy left to go back into the living room with Mom, I flopped down on my stomach and lay listlessly across my bed. That Lori-dori Mermaid song kept running through my mind—I couldn't make it stop. I turned to stare into my aquarium, and felt my usual automatic envy of my fish and their slippery, uncomplicated lives.

And that's when the plan came into my head, so suddenly and forcefully it jolted me bolt upright on my elbows.

Instead of simply envying my fish, why couldn't I become one? Here I'd been calling school "my life," when, if I stopped to think about it, it took up only one-third of my time. School wasn't something I could control, but the other two-thirds of my life was! I could live for eight and one-fourth hours a day in the dry, harsh school world if I knew I would be returning for the bulk of my time to an exciting, mysterious place where I would fit in easily and gracefully!

If I seriously wanted to be a mermaid, all I had to do was turn my room into the ocean!

It was so simple I couldn't believe I hadn't thought of it before. Relief flooded through me. I slid to the floor and spent several hours scribbling out plans on notebook paper.

I went to sleep that night feeling happy for the first

19

time, really, since the popular girls first started noticing Louise.

★ ★ ★

By morning, the details of my plan were clear in my head. I saw that the whole thing basically hinged on whether or not I could talk Mom into letting me redecorate my room.

I knew my best bet would be to catch her in the kitchen, where she's generally in a good mood. So I waited till after school, and sauntered in, trying to act casual, while she was fixing dinner.

"Mom, I've been thinking. I'm going to turn over a new leaf, closetwise, I mean."

I knew that would get her. She's always on me to shovel out my closet. She looked up from the batter she was stirring and raised her eyebrows, pleased.

"And also, I'm going on a whole room campaign, to keep things nicer, you know? So could I paint it? My room?"

I held my breath. My whole fate was riding on her answer. She held out the stirring spoon for me to sample, but I shook my head, too nervous. She tasted it herself.

"What color?" she asked.

"Uh, blue," I answered.

"A very light blue? Nothing like blueberry blue, I should hope."

Deepest sea blue, I thought. Midnight ocean blue.

"A light blue, Mom." That wasn't exactly lying. In science we learned that everything is relative, and ocean blue was definitely lighter than, say, black. Besides, she'd have to love it when it was done. Who wouldn't love walking into a gorgeous seacave, where the harsh light from the glaring surface world was nothing but a dim and distant memory?

"Well, Lori, if your father thinks it's all right . . ."

Home free! Daddy would be so relieved to see me busy and not moping that he would immediately assume I'd latched onto one of those high points he'd explained to me about and would let me do anything I wanted if it would keep me up there and out of the dread seventh-grade pit!

"Thanks, Mom!" I cried happily, bouncing up so quickly the plastic sort of stuck to my jeans and the barstool crashed to the floor. "Can I go to the hardware store now to pick out the paint?"

But she was shaking her head, a no-nonsense look on her face, and when she spoke I knew there was no point in arguing with her. It was the one thing she wouldn't let anyone argue about, ever.

"Absolutely not, young lady. You're not taking a step from this house till you've had some of this good dinner and dessert."

★   ★   ★

So after dinner and coconut pie, Daddy drove me to the hardware store.

"I trust your judgment," he said immediately when I asked if I could go in and pick out the paint myself. He just gave me that soft smile of his, handed me a twenty-dollar bill, and snapped open his newspaper.

I got a gallon of the darkest blue they had—Maritime Navy, it said on the label. The guy who waited

21

on me said it was on sale because people couldn't find anything to use it on.

"Much too dark for decorating use inside, of course. Just slightly too light to pass for black or folks'd buy it to paint their motors and such, I guess," he said.

To tell the truth, I felt a little guilty after he said that. But I kept reminding myself how much my parents would have to love it when it was done, if I could just luck out and get it all finished before they saw it.

Chapter 4

The next day was Friday, and right after school I rushed home to start painting.

Boy, that painting was hard. Partly because I had to do the ceiling and floor and windows, too. That paint definitely didn't want to stick to glass or the slick hardwood floor.

A couple of times Mom knocked on the door, but when I told her I wanted to wait and surprise her with the overall effect when I was finished, she accepted that and left me alone. I should have remembered that earlier and not have been worried about her seeing the room too soon. Mom loves surprises.

I only let myself sleep a few hours Friday night. Sleeping wasn't a hard thing not to do anyway, with that paint smell all over the place.

By noon Saturday, after a morning of passionate work, I was sealed inside a dark cube. The man at the store had been sort of wrong saying my Maritime

Navy paint was slightly too light to pass for black. I would definitely have said it passed for black, once it was on all the surfaces of my room. That was all right, though. I had wanted very deep blue, but now that I thought about it, the ocean probably looked more black than blue when you were far inside it.

The way the color of paint turned out to be so perfect seemed to be more like fate than sheer coincidence. I mean, I hadn't actually known I needed this practically black color, but had gotten it accidentally and it turned out to be perfect.

A contest seemed in order.

"I, Lori Sumner, have parents who weren't crazy about my using dark paint, and at this very moment aren't expecting anything darker than, say, baby blue," I said solemnly, sitting cross-legged on my bed inside the ocean darkness. "When they see this room, if they don't faint dead away I will take that as a very strong sign that I was meant to do this, from some deep Piscean longing too mysterious even for me myself to fully understand."

That "Piscean longing" thing had sounded good! I hadn't known I was going to say it, even, until it came out of my mouth. I had thought a lot about the word Piscean, though, ever since our science teacher, Mr. Landers, told us it meant fishlike in some ancient language.

★　★　★

I spent Saturday afternoon cutting fish out of colored paper and taping them to the walls. I even made one large octopus whose tentacles extended around one corner and up onto the ceiling. A nice touch, I thought. I made a mobile, too, from my shell collection. It hung over my bed within touching distance.

And then I had another brainstorm, and I went into the den and rummaged through Daddy's old record collection until I found "Victory at Sea." I borrowed it, took it to my room and put it, ready to play, on my stereo. My world would not only look like the sea now, but would sound like it, too.

Everything was perfect, and I figured I might as well get my parents' reaction over with. I put the needle on the record and went to find them in the living room.

"Mom? Dad? It's done," I announced.

Dad lowered his paper, shoved his glasses up into his wiry hair, and smiled across the room toward my mother.

"Well, Martha, it's done," he said.

"Okay." She smiled, clapped her hands, tossed her unfinished afghan aside, and stuck it happily with her crochet needles. She just loves a surprise. "Then let's have a look!"

"Remember, it might not be exactly what you expect. But it's my room, after all," I explained, following them nervously down the hall. "Okay? Will you remember? Please? Promise?"

Mom got there first. I heard a small grunt of sound come out of her. Kind of like a little "uh." Then she repeated herself.

"Uh. Oh, Stan. Uh."

My dad looked over her shoulder, then gently moved her aside. She seemed frozen there, filling the doorway.

He looked around the room, then looked around again. His head moved on his neck like a bird's head, probably following the wild curves of the octopus tentacles.

"Black, Lori?" he whispered, turning toward me with absolutely no expression on his face. He moved one finger to push his glasses up on his nose, discovered they weren't there, and put his hand on his cheek instead. "Black?"

Disappointment throbbed all through me.

"You don't like it," I accused them.

Mom turned to look at me, wide-eyed, and moved her mouth soundlessly a few times. Then she turned again and ambled down the hall, like a sleepwalker.

"Uh," I heard her say.

"Honey, if you like it, I like it," Daddy said softly, putting an arm around my shoulders and squeezing me. "Mom will get used to it, except maybe for the floor. And windows."

★ ★ ★

I went to bed a little while after that, but I didn't go to sleep. I just lay there with my heart beating fast. At midnight I got back up to officially complete things.

With my sand candle burning and all the lights off, I solemnly left my human name behind, to be used only artificially when I temporarily had to go through the motions of existence on earth.

My real name, taken that night, became Lorelei, the name of a legendary sea siren who lured sailors to their deaths solely by the power of her ravishing beauty and her mysterious song.

Chapter 5

Monday, of course, I had to leave my watery realm, assume my ungainly land body again, and go to school.

And I innocently and unsuspectingly walked right into trouble.

Somebody was sitting in my place in the gym, leaving me nowhere but right out in the open to sit! A girl with long skinny legs and long stringy brown hair was sitting in the little roofed corner of the gym where I always sat!

I told myself it wasn't that important. I told myself that now that I was a sea dweller, nothing could affect me that much here on dry land. So what if everyone would stare at me if I had to sit out in the open instead of under the little roofed corner where I always sat? So what if everybody would see how alone I was, how fakey my pretending to study looked? So what if

Louise was able to look down with pity and disgust at me from her place with the popular kids?

What did I, graceful Lorelei, care what these ignorant two-legged creatures with their small land brains thought?

But I couldn't take it. I just couldn't sit out there in the open, so I went to ask the stranger in my place to move.

"Excuse me," I said politely, "but I believe this is my seat."

She had on a short skirt, not fashionably short but outgrown short, and she had one leg crossed over the other. Her knees looked crusty, dirty. She swung the crossed leg wildly, and sat slumped with one elbow in the other hand. She had something on a long chain around her neck, and she was clicking it against her teeth.

She acted like she hadn't even heard me—just kept on staring through her tangled, greasy bangs toward the middle of the gym floor, looking at nothing, clicking that thing on the chain.

"Excuse me," I said again, "but I always sit here."

She raised her eyes to me without moving her head, then lowered them to the seat.

"Don't see your name on it," she said, then went on clicking. Her voice was gross and croaky, like a boy's.

I felt my neck sweating, and I knew my hair would be sticking to it and frizzing up in back. I glanced, in spite of myself, up toward where I knew Louise was sitting. She sort of half smiled, like in sympathy, and I bent toward the stranger, shaking all over.

"Please," I choked out, "I've been sitting here since sixth grade. Can't you at least scoot over? There's room enough for two people under here."

The stranger uncrossed her legs, then recrossed them, the other one on top. There was a red mark through the crust on her left knee now.

"You know Morse code?" she asked.

I thought maybe she'd let me sit if I did.

"Sure," I lied.

And sure enough, she inched over a little, and I plopped gratefully down. I was out of sight of the rest of the people in the gym, finally. I closed my eyes and tried to breathe right and quit shaking.

"Okay, then what's this?" she asked, and began tapping out an irregular pattern of clicks against her teeth with that thing on the chain.

I put my elbows on my knees and bent over with my head in my hands, still trying to get my heart to quit banging.

Her sharp elbow in my ribs blasted me upright.

"Hey, that hurt!" I half whispered, half howled.

"I'll do it once more, and listen up this time," she said. "I'm not going to repeat this all day."

Clickety, clickety, click-duh, click-duh, click. I couldn't believe she was sticking such a probably filthy thing in her mouth. In fact, I couldn't believe her at all. I'd seen some weird things in my twelve years as a land animal before becoming a sea creature, but this took the cake.

"Who are you, anyway?" I asked.

"Is that your guess?"

"Huh?"

"Okay, you're right, pretty much anyhow. The answer was Vern. V-E-R-N. I was tapping out my very own name—Vern. I could do Hittlinger, too, but that might take some time."

Vern. I thought that was a boy's name, but she did look like a boy, sort of. Tall and skinny with scabby-looking elbows and knees. But mostly, she had that thing about her that I've noticed boys have. That way of just nonchalantly doing things like walking up and sitting down in a person's place like they own the gym.

"I'm new, in case you're wondering," this Vern person said.

New to this planet, or just to this school? I wondered.

Chapter 6

~~⟶ "I'm originally from the forty-fourth star in the constellation Cassiopeia," she went on, as though reading my mind.

I just looked at her. What do you say to something like that? My math and history books and the little plastic box I keep my pencils in slid from my lap to the floor. The plastic box crashed open and all my junk scattered everywhere.

"Hey, just kidding!" she laughed, bending to help me pick things up. "You looked like you actually believed me there for a second. In fact, it's highly unlikely that there are even that many stars in Cassiopeia. I'd say twenty, tops."

"Why'd you say it, then?" I hissed at her. "I mean, that was a pretty weird thing to say."

"Yeah," Vern immediately agreed. Then she sighed, and shrugged, and sat clicking that thing

31

on her teeth faster and faster until the bell finally rang.

★ ★ ★

I practically ran from the gym to my first class, hoping Vern wouldn't try to latch on to me out of desperation, being a new kid and all. Sometimes new people do that, then drop you when they make real friends they like better. I'm what you could call an expert on the ways people can find to drop friends. Before Louise, there was this kid named Krissi I was best friends with from kindergarten through third grade who ended up dropping me when this girl she liked better moved next door to her. Krissi moved to another town in fourth grade anyway, so it wouldn't have worked out for us to stay friends even if she'd kept liking me.

Still, I think of her sometimes and remember how I felt the first day I watched her and Cindy on the handwalkers all during recess. It was the same kind of empty feeling I had when I found out that Louise had moved out of our locker.

Anyway, I practically ran to my first class to avoid this new Vern character, but halfway to my locker her flat, low voice stopped me.

"You got math first period?" she asked, practically yelling.

She turned out to be right at my heels, almost stepping on them, in fact. When I turned around in the crowded hall, she ran smack dab into me. My face came about to the level of that metal thing hanging around her neck. And standing up, she looked so skinny that I realized we must be about the same

32

weight. You could have taken me and stretched me about another foot and had her.

"No, history," I mumbled, flustered because people were watching, edging past to their lockers and, it looked to me like, snickering at us. The long and the short of it, they were probably thinking. The fat and the skinny. The class joke and the class joke-in-training. "Excuse me, I've got to hurry."

"I've got history, too. I'll walk you," Vern said.

Then why had she asked if I had math? Weirder and weirder.

★   ★   ★

She sat in the empty seat across the aisle from me. I kept hearing her click that metal thing against her teeth while I was trying to concentrate on the Civil War. I felt like yanking it off her neck and dropkicking it to China.

She kept staring out the window, too, looking toward the mountains. That made me think she wasn't from Arkansas. New people are always bowled over by our mountains.

Near the end of the hour, Mr. Parkins brought a new pupil enrollment card back to her and asked her to fill it out before she left the room.

The minute he put the white index card on her desk and walked away, the clicking stopped so abruptly it about deafened me. When it didn't start again, I snuck a look her way.

She had both elbows on the desk and her forehead in both hands, which pushed her greasy hair up into a wild tangle. She was staring down at the card. She looked drained and pale, more like Mr. Parkins had just handed her a live grenade than a simple little enrollment card.

"What's the matter?" I whispered across the aisle to her. "You better hurry and fill that thing out. The bell will ring in a couple of minutes."

She looked up at me and shook her head.

"I hate these," she whispered back to me. Her eyes were red-rimmed. I hadn't noticed that about her before.

"What?" I whispered again. "It's just a stupid little address card, for Pete's sake. Just fill it out. This will be your homeroom, so they need you to fill out the card. It's no big deal, just do it!"

But she just sat there, and pretty soon, sure enough, the bell rang. I thought she'd hang around, waiting to see what my next class was, latching temporarily on to me again.

But when the bell rang, she was out of there.

She ran for the door, leaving the card blank on her desk. Beside it was a sheet of notebook paper that she'd evidently been doodling on when she wasn't gawking out the window at the mountains.

Not that I was much interested, but I figured I might as well pick it up and save it for her. It was covered with tiny stars—stars joined into patterns by delicate straight lines.

Constellations, that's what they were. One, shaped like a "W," was done darker, traced over a bunch of times.

Well, maybe she really was from Cassiopeia after all. She certainly acted strange enough.

★   ★   ★

34

I didn't see Vern the rest of the day, or at least until my study hall last hour. That was when I asked Miss Tarkley for permission to go to the gym and look for my protractor. I hadn't been able to find it in my plastic supply box when I needed it in math, so I figured it was still on the gym floor where all my junk had fallen that morning.

When I pushed open the heavy double doors, that same mysterious feeling surrounded me that I'd had the other day when I was there after school, looking for my purse. Something about the afternoon light coming golden and dim through the high windows made it seem like that, I guess. That, and the total quietness, so weird when you were used to yelling in there and balls and feet pounding.

When the doors whooshed shut behind me, I thought I was alone. But then I saw movement out the corner of my eye, and my heart jumped to my throat. In the corner where the gymnastic team practiced, somebody was on the flying rings. Somebody was swinging high and fast, pumping hard to go even higher and faster.

It was Vern!

I edged quickly behind the bleachers, not wanting her to see me. And I just stood there and watched her for a while. She was good. Real good. She could do most of the tricks the gym team did, even though she was wearing that short skirt and it must surely have cramped her style. Then, as I kept watching, she did a somersault in the air off the rings, and when she landed she ran over to the hanging rope and climbed like a spider clear to the ceiling. She just stayed up there like that, looking around at all the girders and skylights like she enjoyed the view.

Like she belonged in the sky.

It made me dizzy to watch her. I decided I didn't need that protractor all that bad after all, not bad enough to have to talk to Vern. When I thought she was looking in the opposite direction from the doors, I slipped out as quietly as I could.

★　★　★

At home, I grabbed the snack Mom had laid out for me—a slice of peach pie—slathered on a little whipped cream from the fridge, and went quickly to my room.

It was as wonderful returning to my underwater lair after school as I had thought it would be. I could feel my clumsy land body slipping away as I glided into the darkness. I could barely see the shapes of my fellow sea creatures through the comforting gloom of the cool depths. I settled on the floor beside the fish tank to eat and talk to my fish.

Actually, I've never been in the habit of talking to all my fish. Mostly I just talk to my giant angel fish, Louise.

"Louise, this first day with the land creatures was nerve-wracking," I confided. "After only one weekend as a mermaid, I'd already forgotten how tough life is above the surface."

I sighed and ate my pie, as Louise pressed her face up against the glass and watched me, fluttering and gulping.

"A new girl followed me around, at least for a while," I told her, licking my thumb. "I think she just needed a temporary friend, know what I mean? And even if she did want to be permanent friends, well, don't take this wrong, okay Louise? I mean, I'm not a snob or anything. But she's kind of . . . I don't know. Kind of scuzzy. She's got scabby elbows and knees and dresses funny. And talks weird. Super weird. Thinks she's from outer space or something."

While I told Louise that, for a second I saw myself clearly reflected in the aquarium. Usually in my aquarium reflection I have long, flowing sea-hair and look graceful and semi-thin. But I guess I was too close that day. In the aquarium I saw my wiry, fluffy hair, plastered pretty much to the sides of my chubby face. My mouth was chewing, chewing, and my chin was greasy from pie crust. Tiredness washed over me like a wave, and I felt suddenly so sad and discouraged I could hardly move.

"Or maybe I just wouldn't want to be friends with anybody desperate enough to be friends with me," I told Louise.

I crammed the last bite of pie into my mouth and pushed my empty plate out of sight under the bed, then threw myself back on the hard, black floor. Far above me, the shell mobile twirled slowly in the gloom like one of Vern's sad and distant constellations.

Chapter 7

I wondered if Vern would be in my seat again in the gym the next morning, and sure enough, she was.

As I came near her, she held up my protractor proudly and smugly, like it was solid gold or something instead of just costing 45 cents when it was new, which it definitely wasn't any longer.

"Thanks," I said, snatching it and sitting down. At least she'd left room for me this time.

"I found it," she announced. "Under the bleachers. I always find things. I'm a finder."

I smiled a little, politely, trying not to stare at her skirt, which I couldn't help noticing was the same one she'd worn yesterday. A different T-shirt, but the same outgrown skirt.

Nobody at Greenpoint Middle School wears clothes two days in a row. No girls, at least.

"Aren't you gonna ask me what a finder is?"

I shrugged. At least if she was talking, she wasn't clicking. And it surely couldn't be too long till bell time.

"Okay, what's a finder?"

By way of answering, she grabbed the grimy metal thing on the chain around her neck and stuck it in my face.

"I found this," she announced in an excited whisper. "It's a key, see? Somewhere, there's a house that it unlocks."

Sure enough, it was a key. One of those keys that will open practically anything. My grandparents have an old house that used keys like that in every door. Skeleton keys, they called them. Long, skinny, and useless because you could get them at any hardware store in the world. My parents finally made my grandparents change the locks and get real, modern keys.

I started to tell her that, but she was all wound up and I couldn't get a word in edgewise.

"Somewhere there's an elegant Victorian mansion, waiting deserted and lonely," she whispered urgently into my face. "All I have to do is find it, insert this key, and the house will open to me. To me, and to me alone, because I found the key, see? There, I'll have gardens, and a telescope in a turret window. And three bathrooms, all with tubs. And even a television set."

"Even a television set? But everybody has . . ."

"I've found other things. I found the gas cap when my father forgot to screw it back on after getting gas one night. I walked along the side of the road in the pitch darkness, and found it with one bare foot, which was pretty amazing if you stop to think about it. I've found car keys that fell beside the seat. Just reached down, as if my fingers knew where they were. I found a dollar once lying on the ground at the Kansas City Zoo. But this . . ."

She shoved that silly key practically up my nose, and I leaned back to avoid it.

"This is the reason for my finding. All the other finding was practice, leading up to this. I keep this key with me always, because I never know when the house will come along, will just appear, waiting for me. The key was the hard part. Finding it, I mean. Now all I need is the lock."

I sat there nodding, impressed in spite of myself.

She was right—it was pretty amazing that she'd found that gas cap with her bare foot, when you stopped to think about it.

★   ★   ★

We walked together to history—she just seemed to expect I'd want to walk with her, and I couldn't think of any particular reason not to. When we got to class she started staring out the window at the mountains again, like she was in a trance or something. At one point she actually turned to me and whispered hoarsely across the aisle.

"We could go climbing, up Hackberry Slope."

Not "would you like to" or even "maybe we can go sometime." Just "we could go"—how do you answer somebody who doesn't even have the social grace to phrase things right? I couldn't make it even partway up the climbing rope in phys. ed., so I definitely wasn't about to tackle an almost-cliff of a mountain!

But before I could figure out how to get all this firmly across to her, Mr. Parkins brought her another enrollment card.

"Miss Hittlinger, don't forget this this time," he said sternly. "The school requires this information."

I braced myself for her to make a scene, but there was none of the panic I'd seen come over her the day before. She calmly slid the pencil out of the spiral of her history notebook, and began nonchalantly filling out the card. When she'd finished, she walked up and put it on Mr. Parkins's desk.

I saw three of the girls on the front row—Julie Andersen, Cheryl Hopkins, and Pattie Westfall—hunching together to whisper and giggle at Vern. Whether at her skirt or her scabby knees or her greasy hair it was hard to tell. Probably about everything.

It crossed my mind that when Vern had been here a while longer, she'd learn not to draw attention to herself by doing things like walking up to a teacher's desk in the middle of class. She'd learn ways to keep the girls like Julie and Cheryl and Pattie—and even Louise, now—from noticing her much. Maybe I ought to try and give her some pointers about things like that.

Then again, maybe I ought to try harder to lose her before she really got the idea I liked her.

Two things were swirling around inside me—pity for Vern, and embarrassment at the fact that people were already starting to think I was her friend.

The best way to cope with this situation was probably to keep remembering that everything at school was only an unimportant part of my new and real life beneath the sea.

★　★　★

Tuesday and Thursday and Friday are phys. ed. days, which is why I always dreaded them more than other days. All the seventh grade girls have gym together, so Vern was there for the first time that Tuesday. And that first day she was there happened to be a rope climbing day.

When we lined up by the rope, I got as far back in line as I could, my usual practice although I've never lucked out and been saved by the bell. Vern had been farther up in line, but when she saw me she waved and came to stand right behind me.

We bring shorts and T-shirts from home for phys. ed., and when they get too grungy we take them home and wash them. I've got a really huge yellow T-shirt I use, that pretty much covers the worst part of my thighs. Vern was wearing a tight T-shirt that said CARDS across the front, and a pair of those skimpy little shorts they sell for a couple of dollars at Wondermart. They barely covered her bottom.

"My brother's," she said, when she saw me frowning at them. "We share."

If I hadn't been such a nervous wreck about the coming rope climbing humiliation, I might have asked her more about that. As it was, I just nodded as if I understood why someone would share shorts and T-shirts with a brother who must, from the looks of the clothes, have been about nine years old.

Everybody made it at least halfway up the rope, as usual.

And then, all too quickly, it was my turn.

My hands were shaking, and I felt cold and sweaty at the same time. I sort of did a little lurch, jumped a little off the floor, grabbed the stupid, clammy rope, and hung there like a sack.

People were giggling. My arms felt filled with fire. My feet became numb. I couldn't breathe. I dropped down, six inches or so, to the floor.

"My wrists are just too weak," I muttered, my eyes on the ground, my head swimming.

"Lori, I have some exercises I want you to try at home," Miss Arklemyer said. "They'll build your arm and back strength."

My head was pounding, but I knew I'd survive this humiliation. I already had, several times.

Still, as I melted back into the line I had an awful thought. Vern would be next to climb! And she was such an expert, she would make me look twice as bad as I already looked! Usually the three or four girls who, like me, couldn't cut the mustard clumped together at the end of the line, so none of us felt quite so stupid. I mean, I was definitely the worst, but there were a couple of others who could only get a couple of feet off the ground. It was a little comforting to share the humiliation. But today, Vern had upset that system by coming to stand behind me! I would be lucky if Miss Arklemyer didn't point out to everybody within earshot the difference between my fat klutziness and Vern's skinny climbing perfection.

I watched—what else could I do? Vern walked toward the rope and took it into her hands. She pulled up, and the tight T-shirt strained across her back. The waistband of her skimpy pants rode down lower on her hips. But her feet didn't leave the ground. She relaxed, rubbed her hands on her pants, then grabbed the rope and strained up again, but still didn't get a centimeter off the ground. She turned with a shrug of defeat to Miss Arklemyer.

"Sorry. I can't," she said, simply.

Miss Arklemyer scratched her forehead with her pencil, looking disturbed. She chewed her lip as she lifted her notebook and made some kind of mark in it.

"I would think, with your upper torso development . . . oh, well, if you can't, you can't," she said with a perky sigh.

Vern stepped back beside me, looking totally calm, though people were giggling at her now.

"Why'd you do that?" I hissed in her ear.

"Why'd I do what?" she asked innocently.

I grabbed her by the front of her shirt and pulled her over to the nearest corner of the gym, out of earshot of the others, who were busy watching the last klutzy girls, hoping to laugh.

"I said, why'd you mess up like that?" I repeated in a harsh whisper. "I saw you yesterday afternoon, in here. You're an expert at this stuff! So why'd you blow it on purpose?"

She took a deep breath, and let it out.

"Why not?" she answered.

I grabbed two handfuls of my hair in exasperation.

"What do you mean why not? Didn't you hear everybody laughing at you? Didn't you feel humiliated, like you just wanted to die or something? What do you mean why not?"

She stood there frowning, maybe thinking. She reached inside her T-shirt, grabbed the key that was around her neck, and started clicking it against her teeth.

Finally, just when I'd decided to wash my hands of her because she wasn't going to answer me, she spoke.

"I don't care what other people think. Just you. I didn't want to show you up and embarrass you."

Now, I'm not all that easily shocked, but that shocked me. I grabbed her by both her arms, and kind of shook her. It was like an elf shaking a cornstalk. She towered above me there, sort of waving around.

"What do you mean you just care about what I think?" I demanded, forgetting to whisper. A couple of girls turned to look at us, and I felt my neck get hot and quieted down. "You gotta care what everybody thinks, whether you want to or not! Believe me, I know! You might not want to care, but you've got to!"

I stopped and listened to how that sounded, and made a quick correction.

"At least, that is, you've got to care while you're at school, here on dry land."

"Huh?" she said, shaking her head in confusion.

"Listen," I tried to explain, swallowing hard. "I appreciate what you just did, but it's stupid to make yourself look bad. You're new here. People around here respect jocks. When word gets around about your athletic ability, you could probably make friends pretty easily."

If you'd do something about your scabby knees, I almost added, but didn't.

She shrugged and looked me right in the eye through her greasy bangs.

"I don't have time," she said simply. "My system is to make one friend, fast. And here, that's you."

Chapter 8

Needless to say, that made absolutely no sense at all. Of course, I was getting pretty used to that with Vern.

"What d'you mean you don't have time? And what kind of a crazy system is making one friend fast?" I asked, confused and perturbed.

But at that second, before Vern could answer, the bell rang.

"Oh, no, I wanted time to wash my hair!" she moaned, pivoting away from me and heading in long strides toward the showers.

I ran after her.

"Hey, you can't wash your hair in the school showers!" I yelled toward where she was already disappearing into the locker room. "That's weird! Nobody does that. You just duck under the water real quick and get off the sweat, or pretend you did if you're too embarrassed to really shower with everybody watching."

"You wouldn't happen to have any shampoo with you, would you?" she asked over her shoulder, pulling off her T-shirt.

"Of course not," I puffed, sitting heavily down on the wooden bench that runs between rows of gym lockers. "Don't be ridiculous."

"I'll just use soap, then," she said. And she ducked into the showers and turned the water on full blast.

"Why don't you wash your hair at home like normal people do?" I asked her.

But I doubt if I would have said anything that rude if I hadn't been sure she couldn't hear over the water noise.

With a sigh, I stripped off my own gym clothes, dressed back in my blouse and jeans, and went on to my next class real quick before Miss Arklemyer could catch me and give me those exercises she had threatened me with.

★   ★   ★

When I got home that day a couple of the paper fish had fallen off my wall, and one long arm of the octopus was loose and swinging down from the ceiling. It was sort of like the octopus was a character in a silly little kid's book, and was waving good-bye to somebody. It ruined the graceful, mysterious effect of the room completely.

By the time I'd finished repairing the damage, I had gotten in a really depressed mood.

For the first time since I'd decided to become a sea creature, I wondered a little if the whole thing was really possible. I mean, if fish were going to come off the wall when you were least expecting it, how could you ever be sure the place was secure? How could you ever expect to shed your everyday disguise and return to your underwater domicile when that domicile could be so easily messed up and made to look stupid by just a little dried out tape that had become unsticky?

I flopped on the bed without even bothering to start "Victory at Sea." I could feel Louise the fish watching me expectantly, but I ignored her, and just stared furiously at the shell mobile.

As it had the day before, it reminded me more of a constellation than of an underwater shell garden, which it was supposed to be. Ever since Vern, I'd had stars a little on the brain.

And that was another thing to be depressed about— Vern.

She had said she was using me for the fast friend in her weird system. This would lead to yet another way of being dropped—I could feel it in my bones. And this time, I wouldn't even be dropped by somebody neat. I'd be dropped by somebody who shampooed in the gym bathroom, using hand soap.

Everything seemed hard, both to figure out, and to live with.

There was a knock on my door, then Mom opened it quietly and stuck her head inside. Somehow, with some kind of mother radar or something, she always knows when I'm down in the dumps.

"Lori Lynn? You okay?" she asked gently. "You didn't take the fudge bars I laid out for you."

"I'm great. Just perfect," I snarled.

She was quiet for a second. I stared miserably at the mobile, while a couple of hot tears tracked down into my ears. I kind of hoped she saw, and would hug me or tell me I had beautiful eyes or something. But it was far too dark in my black room to see a couple of transparent tears. And besides, hugs wouldn't make my problems disappear.

"Well, Sugarlump, you'll feel better after you eat," Mom said then, and quietly left and shut the door.

★   ★   ★

Vern's hair looked strange the next morning.

Stranger than usual, I mean.

It was still greasy, only dry now at the same time. Sounds impossible, but it was true. Greasy in splotches, dry and flyaway in other splotches.

"I've got a confession to make," she told me as I approached and sat down on the bleacher. "I don't really know Morse code."

"Huh?" I asked, trying not to stare at her hair.

"Morse code. I don't really know it, except S-O-S, of course. I just made that up to get you engaged in conversation that first day."

I chewed on my lip and nodded. That didn't surprise me half as much as a bunch of other stuff about her did.

"What about that making one friend fast stuff?" I asked, and for some reason my throat started feeling tight. "Did you make that up, too? I mean, it really doesn't make a lot of sense, no offense. Why would you only have time to just have one friend, and have them fast? Friends aren't like hamburgers, or something. You don't just go to a fast-friend place, like you'd go to a fast-food place, you know? The whole thing sounds pretty weird to me, if you want to know the truth."

She didn't answer. She just sat there, staring at me, not even clicking her key against her teeth.

I swallowed hard.

"I mean, not that it's any of my personal business, because it's not," I went on to fill the awful quiet. "I'm not saying I'm offended or anything, or worried about being dropped by you, or anything. Because it's not like we're even what you'd call official friends. Just because you messed up on the rope."

Still, she didn't speak. She moved her eyes from me to her lap, and started chewing one thumbnail, frowning.

I drew my breath in, and let it out hard.

"Listen," I said. "What I really want to tell you is that I'm not exactly what you would call desperate, you know? I mean, you might have gotten that mistaken impression, but just weeks ago Louise Hartley and I were best friends. So I'm not some little nobody or anything like that that needs your sympathy, okay?"

She raised her eyes then, but her shoulders looked slumped.

"So you don't want to be friends," she said, with that flat, low voice of hers. "I guess that means you don't even want to climb Hackberry Slope with me."

And she got up and started walking right across the gym and out the big double doors into the main part of the school. Honestly! Right in front of everybody, before the bell had rung, she just left like that! A thing that wasn't allowed at all by the administration, and looked really stupid besides!

You could hear shock waves rippling, in the form of giggles, throughout the entire bleachers.

Chapter 9

So I had no idea what to expect when I got to history.

Vern might have been apprehended by one of the teachers monitoring the halls, and might be in the office or somewhere getting bawled out for not staying in the gym till first bell rang like you were supposed to. Or, if she'd managed not to get caught in the halls, still she might cut class. Or if she was in class, she might purposely sit clear across the room from me.

But there she was when I walked in, sitting in her usual place right next to where I always sat.

"Mad?" I asked, pretty calmly I thought, considering her strange behavior.

She didn't answer. She didn't look mad, she didn't look friendly. She just looked blank. She had a piece of paper out and was drawing, stars and lines again. Constellations.

"Okay, then, suit yourself," I whispered, sliding into my desk. "Just be mad."

She looked toward me when I said that, then looked back down at her paper, frowning. There were little flecks of something all over her shoulders. Dried soap, I guessed. Too big for dandruff.

I was glad to see that. Something about it made the heaviness that had settled in my chest loosen up a little. How bad could it be to lose a friend who wasn't really a friend yet anyway, and had gross dried shampoo junk all over her stretched out navy blue T-shirt?

I shoved my books under my seat and was rummaging through my supply box for a pencil, when Mr. Parkins's shadow fell across my desk. I looked up to see him bending over Vern, waving her little white card under her nose and whispering furiously. Like the rest of the class, I strained to hear.

"There is no Elm Street in Greenpoint, young lady!" he was saying. "No Elm Street, and no such phone number as 2021! Now, I don't know why you would think it was clever to give false information on your enrollment card, but I assure you, such insolent behavior will simply not be tolerated! At your last school they might have thought such pranks were humorous. However, here at Greenpoint we take an entirely different . . ."

Vern interrupted him, her voice deadly dull. Duller, lower, flatter than usual, even.

"There's always an Elm Street," she said. "Every town has an Elm Street."

Mr. Parkins straightened up and crossed his arms. I could tell he was trying to make some sense of that.

I could have warned him to save his brain power. Very little that Vern said or did, in my opinion, made much sense.

Everybody had heard at least part of what was going on, and everybody was starting to whisper and giggle. As Mr. Parkins turned his attention from Vern to the rest of us, ready to clamp down on our noise, Vern grabbed up the card he had put on the edge of her desk. She quickly tore it in half, then headed like a tall, skinny missile right out the door. It happened so fast the two parts of the torn card were still circling in the breeze she'd left behind her when she was out of sight. They finally fell to the floor, along with the constellation picture she'd left on her desk.

Well, there was shocked silence then. All of us, Mr. Parkins included, just stared at the empty doorway. Then the whole class turned, like one twenty-four-headed monster, toward Mr. Parkins.

He cleared his throat and shut his mouth, which had been partway open. His neck looked splotchy.

"Open your books to section fourteen, The Beginning of Reconstruction," he said in a no-nonsense voice, walking briskly up to his desk. "And remember, folks, our task in here is the study of history, not the study of our friends' and neighbors' problems."

While everybody opened their books, quiet for a change because of what had just happened, I reached down and picked up the half of Vern's enrollment card that had landed on the floor by my left foot. "Pupil Name: Vernita Hittlinger, Pupil Address: 106

Elm Str . . ." That's all there was on that half of the card.

So, Vern's real name was Vernita.

I glanced over to be sure Mr. Parkins wasn't watching our side of the room, then quickly stretched down and retrieved Vern's star drawing paper from the floor. Mr. Parkins had accidentally stepped on it on his way back to his desk.

It looked a lot like the other one I'd seen, the paper she'd drawn on Monday, only it was more detailed like she'd worked on it for hours. The intricate lines, the tiny overlapping shapes with their sharp star-cornered angles—you had to think her sky map was beautiful. This time, she had a bunch of the constellations labeled. Orion. Ursa Minor. Andromeda. Cassiopeia (that one, the W-shaped one, was in the darker print). Pisces.

Pisces? The ancient name for fish? I hadn't known till that very second that there was a fish constellation, and something about that really got to me. I closed my eyes and saw my shell mobile turning in my dark room like a constellation.

I turned over Vern's poor crumpled sky map and carefully began wiping Mr. Parkins's footprint off the back.

Chapter 10

I went looking for her after history, to return her sky map.

I had a hunch where she'd be, especially since it was Wednesday and there were no gym classes on Wednesday mornings.

When I pushed open the big double-doors of the gym, that quiet, mysterious feeling hit me again like it had the other times I'd been in there when it was empty. And then I let my eyes focus to the darkness a little, and peered across to the gymnastics corner.

Sure enough, there was a shadowy shape huddled at the top of the hanging rope, looking at home up there in what she could reach of the sky.

I took my shoes off and walked across the basketball court to stand under the rope.

"You can tell me to leave if you want to be alone," I called up to her. My voice sort of echoed in the emptiness.

She didn't answer.

"I've got your constellation paper. It's beautiful," I said, lowering my voice a little. No echo this time. "Really, it is. I draw, too. Fish, though."

The bell rang. It was the bell to start second period. I'd already decided to cut—I'd only cut class once before, the afternoon Louise left our locker. But this seemed like an emergency.

"You're going to be late," Vern said quietly from the ceiling.

"Yeah," I agreed. "I'm not going, though, so no big deal."

"Why not?" she asked.

"I dunno," I said, and shrugged. "Because I want to tell you something, I guess."

"What?"

I thought about that.

"I guess I don't really know," I admitted, suddenly totally exhausted and confused. My neck was getting sore from craning up into the shadowy girders, trying to see her. I went over and sat on the floor by the bleachers, leaned back against them, and closed my eyes. For the third or fourth time that day, I felt all tangled around inside like I almost wanted to cry. Maybe I was just hungry—that's what my mother would have guessed. But I'd had my usual huge breakfast.

Vern suddenly slid quietly about halfway down the rope. Amazingly, she hung there by one hand, and picked up her key necklace and began clicking it against her teeth with the other hand.

"Okay, I remembered what I wanted to tell you," I

said, hoping my voice wasn't shaking. I sure did wish I had a candy bar or something. "It's just that . . . well, I don't think you should have to tell Mr. Parkins or anybody else your real address or phone or even your real name unless you want to. I mean, I actually go by a false name here at school myself."

I waited for her shocked reaction to that. But she didn't move, except for her fingers, which still kept tapping her teeth with that key. Of course, the rope was swaying a little, so she was sort of slightly moving in the air like a bird on a sideways telephone wire.

"Everyone here knows me as Lori. But my real name is Lorelei. Perhaps you've heard of the graceful, ancient siren who lured sailors to destruction with her enchanting beauty."

It had cost me a lot of turmoil to reveal that. Actually, I'd never planned to share that information with anyone. It made her stop her clicking, but she still didn't budge.

"My real name is Vernita," she said.

Then, she jerked her head quickly toward the doors, listening.

"Somebody's coming!" she hissed, and scampered back up the rope to the ceiling quick as a Yo-Yo jerked back into a hand.

"Hey!" I hissed back, outraged at being left alone like that to face whatever music was coming. There was definitely somebody just outside the big double-doors, all right, pushing against them.

And then, Miss Arklemyer bounced into the gym, her usual perky self. She started toward her office by the locker room, then saw me and made a beeline straight toward me.

"Looking for me, Lori?" she asked, putting her hands on the hips of her crisp khaki shorts. Then she raised one thin, muscular arm and wagged a finger in my face. "Ohhh! I promised you an exercise plan, now didn't I? Just a sec—I'll get it."

As she ducked into the locker room, I looked daggers up at Vern. But I didn't dare speak—Miss Arklemyer was still just feet away, and her hearing was as perky as the rest of her.

"Here we go!" she said, smiling with about two hundred white teeth as she came back into the gym. "Now, I want you to do these exercises for about thirty minutes daily, to start. Concentrate on the push-ups and sit-ups. They'll not only develop arm and back strength, but will increase your overall fitness. O-kay? Okay, then! Go for it!"

And with a slap on my back that I guess was meant to pack about a ton of encouragement, she jogged away.

I looked down at the fat exercise manual she'd left in my hands. Even holding it made my arm muscles ache.

I glared up at Vern, too mad to do anything but squint my eyes and shake my head at her menacingly.

When she was sure Miss Arklemyer was safely in her office, Vern slid down the rope, landing with a soft thud a couple of feet from where I stood.

I was furious, but she looked at me innocently and just shrugged.

"Why'd you just leave me alone like that?" I

exploded. "Why didn't you come down the stupid rope instead of going back up like that, leaving me deserted and getting me stuck with this gross exercise plan that will probably kill me and is just definitely all I need—oh, yeah, just definitely all, all I need—as if my life wasn't a mess enough right now!"

She swallowed then, and her eyes looked red-rimmed again, like they had when Mr. Parkins gave her that first enrollment card. She looked down at the floor and reached for her key.

But I grabbed her skinny wrist.

"So help me, if you start clicking that thing I'll tear your head off," I growled.

She nodded, easily accepting the logic of that, and dropped her hand to her side.

We both just stood there, then. I could tell she felt bad about how things had worked out, so I was trying to cool down and forgive her.

Then suddenly, she looked up and snapped her fingers.

"I know!" she said, brightly and happily as if she'd just discovered the formula for chocolate. "I could go home with you and sit on your feet!"

I just looked at her blankly, still a little mad and confused now, too.

"You know," she said, "sit on your feet while you do the sit-ups and push-ups! It would make it a lot easier. And we could work on your endurance by hiking Hackberry Slope! I could be like your coach. Ropes, mountains—I know about that stuff."

"Oh, yeah?" I said, hoping she wasn't too weird

not to know sarcasm when she heard it. "Like you knew about Morse code, right?"

But I smiled just a little, accepting her offer.

She was right. No matter how scabby, greasy, and weird Vern was, she knew more than anybody I'd ever met about sky stuff.

Chapter 11

So that's how Vern and I ended up sneaking out of the school during the middle of second period that day, heading to my house so she could start making me into a rope climber.

I thought I'd better prepare her a little for my room, and I knew that wouldn't be easy without getting into a tricky explanation about my secret life as a fish. I was kind of walking silently, looking at my feet and wondering how to start explaining, when she asked me something so strange it broke my concentration completely.

"Tell me, Lorelei. Do you believe in gravity?"

I thought she was joking, of course, and looked up from my feet ready to laugh. But she was dead serious. She was looking solemnly up at where a jet was leaving a sharp white line across the late-fall blue of the sky. She moved her eyes back and forth, like she

63

was trying to see if the amount of sky was equal on each side of the white dividing line.

"Don't be embarrassed if you do believe in gravity," she said matter-of-factly, peeling her eyes from the jet trail and putting them on me. "Lots of people do. Here on the earth, with stuff pulling at your feet all the time, it's hard not to."

"Here on earth?"

"As opposed to in the sky, I mean. When you're in the sky, like on a mountain or the flying rings or something, you push easily through things. There aren't any tracks or roads or walls or ceilings, so you can go in any direction. No rules, no expectations. No enrollment cards. When you look at things from the sky you start to see that gravity and all the problems that come from being stuck to the ground just don't really have to exist."

I meant to set her straight, to tell her that a million scientists couldn't be wrong about gravity just because she had some weird hang-up about doing her enrollment card. But instead, I heard myself saying something completely different.

"It's like that in the oceans, too," I whispered. "No gravity. You push easily through, and the darkness gives way, just softly opens to you, then closes back, without a bunch of hassles over every move you make. Without people thinking things about you and laughing at you behind your back and stuff. The sea is just soft darkness, and you gliding easily through it."

"Yeah," she agreed, like she really did understand. "And the sky is huge. You could travel through it forever. If you think about that, you see that every place is your home, you know? I mean, because every place you stop has the same sky and the same stars at night. Kind of like furniture that you're used to. That you actually own."

"On the other hand, the ocean is so huge that no place has to be your neighborhood," I added excitedly. I'd never been able to talk about stuff like this to anyone but Louise the fish! "I mean, fish can't get close friends, because they're so slippery and alike. They just can't, see? Say a fish had a close friend one day—well, by the next day she wouldn't even recognize her, probably. So in the ocean, you shift for yourself and you just don't worry so much about things like having and losing friends."

"Right," Vern said, with a firm nod. "You can only have time for one friend at each place, fast."

Where had I heard that before? I shook it out of my head, too excited about this conversation to stop to think about it now.

"I can't believe we've both thought so much about this same stuff, you know?" I told her breathlessly. "And did you ever stop to think about how in the sea, and probably in the sky, too, you can just be yourself, not what anyone else thinks you should be? Take whales, for instance. Whales never have to climb the whale equivalent of ropes or anything like that. And would you call a whale fat? Pretty silly, huh? Whales are absolutely huge, but they're allowed to be themselves, is what I'm trying to say!"

"Right," she agreed, stopping in the middle of the sidewalk and turning to face me. "Only creatures of the land get called names."

I opened my mouth to agree. But something about the soft, sad way she'd said that last sentence had made my throat so tight I was afraid my voice would come out as a squeak.

So I took a couple of deep breaths, then started walking again, and she followed me.

"You're going to like my room, I think," I told her over my shoulder.

And I felt so good then. Not forced happy, like when you have to smile and pretend you're doing okay when Louise smiles down at you in the gym. But really, comfortably, easily happy. Unalone, for the first time in ages.

But I didn't get to feel that way for long. Maybe about half a block, tops.

I think before I even heard the car squealing up behind us I sort of heard a strangled little sound come from Vern—sort of a desperate, scared "uh-oh."

Then a huge station wagon, about the size of a boat and the color of a bone, appeared from out of nowhere, pulled up to the curb, and stopped so fast it kept rocking back and forth, back and forth. A big man with a dark beard and huge wet stains under both arms jumped out, grabbed Vern by the elbow, and dragged her off the curb. She went limply, her head down.

He kind of shoved her into the backseat of the car, then took the burned down cigarette out of his mouth, threw it on the ground, and stomped it angrily. I had the feeling he would have liked to stomp Vern the same way, and I felt my stomach squeeze into itself and turn over.

I licked my lips. "Vern?" I sort of bleated, scared to death.

The man, who was in the process of hurling himself back into the car, stopped halfway under the steering wheel and fixed me with a hot, dark-eyed glare.

"Vernita ain't got no time or no business with you," he said, so quietly it made goosebumps pop out all over me. "Her mother and me have enough problems without that she cuts classes with some hoodlum she meets her first week in school."

Then the man slammed shut the door and the car squealed from the curb. It went wildly down the street, hitting the Meyers' trash can about half a block away.

There was a long, jagged crack in the glass of the back window. The last thing I saw was Vern, on her knees, looking back at me through that cracked glass, slowly waving.

I lifted my eyes to the sky and watched the last of the white jet trail dissolving into the blue afternoon sky.

That trail cut the sky in half the same way the break in that glass cut Vern.

★   ★   ★

I couldn't go back to school. I felt too sick. It was out of the question.

I couldn't do the exercises, either. Way too hard to face.

I just lay on my bed all afternoon, staring at the Pisces mobile.

67

At supper, I kept wanting to tell my folks about what had happened, but I couldn't find the words. That look Vernita's father (I guessed that had been who he was) had given me wouldn't get out of my head. I felt scared all over again when I thought about it. And that thing he'd called me—a hoodlum. It made me feel sort of guilty some way. Guilty of partly causing Vernita's family's problems, whatever exactly they were.

I went to my room right after dinner. I thought maybe that would draw my father to investigate, and sure enough, it did.

"Knock, knock," he said, outside the door.

"What, Daddy?"

"Private party in there, or can anybody crash? Gotta have fins, or will my old snorkel and mask do?"

I rolled my eyes and hurried to open the door.

"Oh, Daddy," I whispered.

And for a couple of seconds I just looked at him, leaning with his shoulder against the doorjamb, his hands deep in his pockets and his face long and skinny. I noticed that his glasses were up there on his head as usual, probably forgotten and pretty much buried in his bushels of wiry hair. I saw the look of worry and love in his gray eyes.

And when I saw all that, I just wanted him to hug me. And when he did, I just stood there crying against him and not even worrying about him being mad because I was soaking his shirt.

There was more chance that the octopus on my wall would come to life than that he would get mad at me for something like that.

"Hey, Lori-dori, don't float away on those tears, okay?" he finally whispered, still holding me. "I don't want to have to call the Coast Guard to retrieve my best girl."

"Oh, Daddy," I whispered back, half laughing, half wincing at his typically crummy joke.

"Want to talk now?" he asked.

I shook my head "no" against him.

So he just shifted a little, and put his arms back around me, tighter. I stood leaning against him for a couple more minutes, and he just stood there letting me.

Chapter 12

⌒**B**oy, did I have some crazy dreams that night. Usually when I go to bed, even after a nerve-wracking day, I can picture myself slipping deeper and deeper beneath the warm waters of a coral atoll in the middle of the Pacific, and that will lull me into a cozy, dreamless sleep. But that night, sleep didn't come easily. And when it finally came, it was like being at the movies.

First, I dreamt of a huge mobile hanging in space. I could tell it was in space, because a bunch of planets (one of them with rings—must have been Saturn) kept whirling by it. Then I saw the word PISCES spelled out in stars at the top of the mobile. It wasn't exactly my shell mobile, though, because I noticed there were people climbing on each string, where the shells were supposed to be. People were climbing easily up and down the strings, dressed in gym shorts. But on one string, somebody hung heavily near the bottom, kicking for all she was worth against the black emptiness of space all around her. You could tell if her weak wrists gave out and she fell, that space blackness would swallow her. Then my mother, dressed like a well-padded version of the good fairy in *The Wizard of Oz,* flew by, waving her wand over the poor kicking person and speaking kindly. "Don't worry, Sweetcakes, it's only your metabolism . . ."

I woke up in a cold sweat, and finally I had to turn on the light and take down my mobile. Only when it was hidden in the closet could I get the dream out of my head and go back to sleep.

But no sooner was I asleep again than I dreamed I was in an old house, alone far back in the woods. I was sitting on the floor of the bathroom. In the bathtub, I had a collection of fish, including Louise. I should have been happy, but something was worrying me. And then I heard footsteps coming up the Victorian staircase in the hall. A moment later the bathroom door crashed open, and Vern was standing there, a towel around her neck. "How do you expect me to wash my hair with all those fish in the way?" she asked. "Hey, if I have greasy hair like this forever, it will be all your fault. All your fault . . ."

Again, I woke up. Not scared this time, just aggravated. Why should Vern's hair be my fault, even in a dumb dream? I socked my pillow to fluff it up a little, and tried to go back to sleep before my brain got all the way awake.

This time, things started off better. I began dreaming I was a mermaid, which is a good way to start the coral atoll feeling that always sinks me deep into sleep. But just as I got too far gone to easily wake back up, I realized I wasn't swimming alone. There was another mermaid swimming with me, right at my tail. Copying all my graceful perfected loops, twirling in and out of wrecked ships as practically my shadow. I turned back to her, meaning to tell her she was invading my part of the sea, but she smiled at me and offered something hidden in her closed hand. She opened her fingers just long enough to give me a quick peek at it, and I saw that it was shining, a rare thing this deep in the ocean. Entranced, I whirled around and reached for it, but she quickly closed her hand. I only caught a glimmer of whatever treasure it was from between her clenched fingers. Because at that moment, a dark shadow passed over our heads, and the water churned menacingly above us. A school of bright tetras darted under a giant clam shell for cover. I looked at her, and she looked back at me in panic and snatched her hand away. We swam together quickly and silently, and cautiously surfaced half a mile or so behind whatever it was that had passed above us.

In the middle distance, against the orange of the dawn horizon, we saw a ship. An ugly ship, square and beige as a bone, quivering as it turned to come back our way. At the wheel was a dark-haired, wild-eyed pirate. As he bore the ship down on us, I could see ugly wet circles under the arms of his torn pirate shirt. He threw the butt of a cigarette into the deep green sea.

And I wanted to dive, to hide in the shadowy seacave crevices only I knew about. But the other mermaid just stared at the pirate, a deep sadness in her eyes. She was frozen there, and I knew it would take precious time I didn't have to pull her down, down with me, into the depths that could hide us. She had offered me what treasure she had, but if I tried to save her I might be hacked to pieces myself . . .

When I woke from that dream, light was leaking through the places I hadn't gotten too well when I painted my windows. I just lay there, wondering what I was feeling, finally deciding it was sadness. I sat up and stretched, expecting the relief you always feel when a nightmare turns out to be just a nightmare.

But relief didn't come. I felt sad all morning, getting dressed and going to school. And when I went to the gym I saw that no one was sitting in Vern's spot.

And really, deep down, that didn't surprise me at all.

★   ★   ★

She wasn't in history, either. When Mr. Parkins called roll, he went right through the "H's" without calling her name.

I raised my hand when he'd finished, though I knew I was inviting giggles from the girls on the front row.

"Mr. Parkins?" I said, when he didn't see me. "Uh, you didn't call Vernita's name."

Sure enough, the girls on the front row giggled. Cheryl even snorted, then they giggled again. Mr. Parkins looked over the tops of his glasses, searching for me.

"I'm aware of that, Miss Sumner," he said, squint-

73

ing in my direction. "Miss Hittlinger dropped out of school yesterday afternoon."

My throat felt dry as a beach all of a sudden, but I forced myself to press on.

"Dropped out?" I asked.

He put his elbows on his desk and pushed the tops of his fingers together.

"Her parents removed her from school, yes," he confirmed. "Presumably, she shall continue her schooling elsewhere. Now, let's turn to page one hundred twenty-six, everyone."

I felt like all the air was being squeezed out of me, and I jumped to my feet, needing to get this straight, no matter what.

"But . . . but where?" I asked.

Mr. Parkins snatched off his glasses and shook his head impatiently in my direction.

"Miss Sumner, take your seat please! There are more important things to be taken up in this class than where Miss Hittlinger intends to study next! And anyway, how could I possibly know where she's going when she refused to even tell us on her card where she was while she was here!"

Now the girls in the front exploded with laughter, bent double in their chairs. The rest of the class laughed along a little, probably figuring any time wasted in history was time well spent.

Mr. Parkins looked flustered, and rubbed his hands down his face, like he usually does when he's trying to figure a plan to get back control of the class.

"I bet she moved back to Pigpen Junction, where she evidently came from!" Cheryl got out between

74

gulping laughs. "Maybe she just got too homesick for her old mudhole. Hey, Lori, you could go visit her there! You'd fit right in—with the oinkers, get it?"

Cheryl really cracked up then, but most of the kids kind of shook their heads and looked uneasy and calmed down a little. I was burning all over, including in my brain, so I couldn't think too well. But I did notice Louise was staring at her desk, and the back of her neck was pink. From laughing?

Oh, please, not from laughing. The thought of that made me feel sick again, like I had the night before when I thought about Vern's father yanking her into his car. I sank into my seat, wishing I could sink right through it, through the floor, through the ground, through the earth, through the universe, into nothingness.

"Miss Hopkins, that will be quite enough. Now class, you will get hold of yourselves and open your books!" Mr. Parkins was saying firmly, though his voice sounded far away and tiny to me.

Other things were rumbling louder inside me, drowning him out. Rumbles of humiliation, rumbles of dread. How would I get through the next five minutes, let alone the next sixty years?

How would I do it, fat like this—an "oinker" without a friend in my corner? Without Krissi from kindergarten, without Louise, without . . . anybody?

And then suddenly Mr. Parkins was at my elbow, bending down to me. His eyes looked funny, and he swallowed a couple of times.

"Uh, Lori, I . . . that is, I wish things hadn't been said that were just said," he whispered, and swallowed again. "That is, I see how hard it is on you, not being able to tell Vernita good-bye. So I've decided to give you her temporary location, though it's my understanding she's moving this next weekend."

He handed me a folded slip of paper, which I quickly folded again and slipped into the pocket of my jeans.

He put a finger to his lips.

"That information is confidential, understand? Given only to myself and the principal yesterday by Vern's father."

"Thanks, Mr. Parkins," I whispered back to him. "I understand, and I won't tell it to a soul."

The rest of the hour was terrible, of course. But not as terrible as it would have been if I hadn't felt Vern's address safe there in my pocket.

I guess that's when I realized that whether I liked it or not, Vern Hittlinger had become my friend.

Chapter 13

The one good thing about totally humiliating class periods is that they always eventually end.

Oinker. The word was an open sore in my mind, and every time I touched it I thought I was going to throw up. But the bell rang to end Mr. Parkins's class, finally. I stayed at my desk and waited for everybody else to leave, not at all up to looking anybody in the eye that had heard me called that word.

When the room was empty I still sat staring at the mountains out the window. I wondered: should I wait till I got home to read Vern's address, or should I try to pry it out of my tight jeans now? I stood up, stuck out my right hip, started slowly excavating into my pocket.

"Lori?"

The voice was a total shock. I jerked at my hand, which was stuck tight in my pocket.

"Hi, Louise. I didn't know you were still here."

She took a step from the doorway, toward me.

"Uh, I got most of the way to math and came back. I just wanted to tell you I was sorry."

"Sorry? About what?" I asked, miserably. I could feel perspiration trickling into the waistband of my jeans.

I shoved my other hand as far as it would go into my other pocket, hoping I looked balanced and casual. I hadn't been alone with Louise since she moved out of the locker, two weeks that seemed more like two years ago. She was so cool now, like the other popular kids. It was hard to believe I had once known how to talk to her, without even thinking about it.

"You know, sorry about what Cheryl said. She just likes to cut up. She . . . she doesn't always think about how she sounds."

"Yeah. It's okay, no biggie. I'll live." I kept gulping, hoping I wouldn't cry.

Louise just stood there, her neck pinkish like she was embarrassed, too. I finally got up the nerve to look in her eyes, and it was then that I saw she probably hadn't really changed that much after all, when you got right down to it. She was still the person who used to be my best friend, though everyone had trouble believing that. You could see it in her eyes—they were still quiet someway, deep.

"You'll never be an oinker," she said then. She smiled and the corners of her mouth trembled. "A mermaid maybe—an oinker, never."

I was dumbfounded. I think my mouth fell open. How did she know? How in the world did she know

I was basically a mermaid now? And then I remembered the part-dream, part-joke we'd shared between us when we were sixth-graders—she would someday turn into Pegasus because she loved horses so much, and I would become a mermaid because I was such a fish fanatic.

"Oh. Oh, yeah." I felt let down. It hadn't been intuition about me like she'd once had, but simple memory. "So do you still love horses?"

She shrugged and turned to start out the door to her next class. "I guess, but I've been too busy lately to think about them much."

I nodded, wishing I could say the same thing. Wishing I could tell her I'd been too busy to think about fish.

"Louise? Thanks for talking to me."

She whirled back around, looking surprised and hurt. For a second I even wondered if she felt like crying, like I did.

"Oh, Lor," she whispered. "You know I miss you, don't you? I still think of you as a friend. I could really talk to you and share things with you, like I've never been able to do with anyone else."

And then she ducked her head and was gone around the corner, practically running.

There's this show on TV about a beautiful girl who has a bunch of friends who are sort of monsters, living underground in a secret community. She likes them better than she likes the cute and popular people above the ground that she lives with and goes to parties and stuff with. But still, she really does have kind of a choice, and she stays above the ground. Which

79

leads you to believe that cute and popular win out over really liking.

I thought about that after Louise left that day.

My fingers were starting to feel numb. I bent back, taking the strain from my pockets, and jerked both hands out. Between my index and middle finger of my right hand I'd managed to grip Vern's address.

"Greenpoint Jaycee Campground," I read. But that didn't make sense.

What kind of an address was that? The Jaycee Campground was a place for the annual bass fishing contest, and for the bikeathon in the spring. It wasn't a place to live, for Pete's sake.

* * *

It was a cold day, of course, being the fourth day of November and everything. I had my down jacket, though, so I decided I could walk the mile or so to the campground. Actually, I didn't have any choice. I could hardly go home and ask my mother to drive me somewhere when I was cutting class for the second time in one single week.

Besides, I needed to think, and the cold clear air felt good, like it was airing out my brain. I just kept wishing my thighs didn't rub together every step I took, like they were flapping out some word or something. Like—oinker, oinker, oinker. My legs started aching about halfway there, but that ache felt good in a way. At least, not as bad as I expected it would.

The campground, when I got there, looked deserted and desolate. In the summer it's pretty, with leaves on the oaks and poplars. It's set in a ring of mountains, some of the tallest around here, including Hackberry Slope.

Hackberry Slope! So that's why Vern had had that on the brain! I realized then she must really be living out here someplace, maybe in a cabin I didn't know about or something.

But where? I worked my way over the rutted entrance road, my ankles twisting and turning, clear to the middle of the campground. I couldn't see a sign of life in any direction. All I saw, partly hidden by a stand of cedar trees, was an old broken-down car someone must have abandoned out there.

And then something clicked in my head—No, wait! That wasn't just any old broken-down car. That was the gross, broken-down car driven by the dark-haired pirate Vern had disappeared with the morning before!

My legs quit aching and got kind of weak feeling. I was scared—scared of that man who was Vern's father, and scared of something else I couldn't name. By then I'd realized there was a thin trickle of campfire smoke rising from near the car. In November? A campfire in November?

I held my breath and shut my eyes, figuring maybe a contest would help.

"I, Lori Sumner, have never been in a deserted campground in the winter before," I began. Then I realized that was all wrong, and started over.

"I, Lori Sumner, have come in search of Vernita Hittlinger," I whispered to the mountains, taking another run at it. "If I don't see any trace of her in the next minute and a half I'll take that as a sign I'm not meant to ever . . ."

"Lorelei?"

I about jumped out of my skin, and jerked my head around so fast my hair hit my face like a gob of frozen cotton.

"Vern? Vern! It's you!"

She was standing about twenty feet from me, over near the creek. She was wearing the skirt and T-shirt she'd worn to school the day before, with thick socks pulled up to the middle of her knees and a gray zippered sweatshirt. In her hands she had a green plastic bucket and an orange towel. She had the strangest look on her face. And after a couple of seconds I understood a whole bunch of things from that look, all of which could be summed up in one sentence.

Vern lived in that awful station wagon.

"Hi, Lorelei," she said. "I was just . . . washing up."

I nodded, trying to act normal though things were churning around a mile a minute in my brain so I could hardly think.

"I was just out walking," I said.

It was her turn to nod. I knew her well enough by then to know that Vern was the kind who could accept the fact that someone would just be out walking in the middle of nowhere in the middle of a schoolday in the middle of winter.

Still, she had that look on her face that I could tell was embarrassment (an emotion I was an expert on) taken to about the one-hundredth degree.

Something needed to be said.

It looked like I would have to say it.

I groped through my mind like somebody groping for a grip on a stupid gym rope, and came up with a thought I would normally have run from as fast as I could.

"Want to climb Hackberry Slope?" I asked, for some reason. I guess because I knew she did want to climb it, in the worst way.

Her eyes lit up like a flashlight had just gone on behind them, and she dropped the green bucket. It hit the gray grass with a little whack, and some water splashed out and started to immediately freeze on the ground.

"Oh, yes!" she answered. Surprise, surprise. "Yes!"

Chapter 14

⟶ "**D**on't you need to tell your mom or anything?" I asked uneasily as Vern dropped the towel beside the bucket and started straight toward the slope.

"Nah," she answered. "Mom's packing to leave, Dad's fishing for dinner. Tyrone can take care of himself."

I glanced over at the car again, trying not to stare. Tiny shapes were moving around it. A thin, slow-moving woman. A little boy with a bright red hat on.

Vern was walking so fast I had to sort of trot to keep up with her.

"Uh, Vern?" I panted. "Where are you moving to?"

That stopped her in her tracks. We'd already started to climb, through the scruffy little knee-high cedars at the bottom of the slope. I put a hand above my eyes, grateful for the break, and looked up at the grayish-blue sky throbbing far away behind the peak of Hackberry Slope. We had a million miles ahead of us, all uphill.

Vern groped around through the layers of shirts she had on for a few seconds, frowning. Finally she gave up and bent over, threw her hair forward, and found the back of her neck chain. She gave it a firm yank, which brought that key of hers scrambling up through her clothing, to about choke her.

I figured she was going to tap her teeth with it, but she didn't. Instead she took it in one hand and yanked it, breaking the flimsy chain. Then she held the key and broken chain out in front of me, looked in my eyes, and spoke huskily and solemnly.

"Lorelei, my mother called her sister in St. Louis yesterday, and it looks like maybe my dad can get his old job back. The car plant has reopened this fall. They think we're moving to St. Louis tomorrow."

She looked down at the key, still extended out toward me.

"They think?" I asked, whispering.

She took a deep breath, looked from the key to the summit of the slope, then back to me.

"My parents think we're moving to St. Louis tomorrow. But I think our new home is waiting, up this mountain. You know, the house I told you about that my key opens. If I can just find it, they'll have to be overjoyed, and they'll have to see this is where we belong. They'll have to know this is home and stay. Lorelei, your coming out here today has given me the hope I'd about lost. Now I truly think that with your help I'll find it."

And then she closed her hand tightly over the key and started climbing again, taking long strides through the rocks and grabbing small trees for leverage with her free hand.

I stood frozen there for a few seconds, trying to understand what she'd just said. Vern was climbing, then, toward a home in the sky. Just as I had plunged into a more comfortable home far under the sea. My plan had been well thought out, though. Carefully followed, so that every detail was taken care of.

I was worried about Vern, on the other hand. She was climbing recklessly, thinking about two seconds ahead, as usual.

"Vern!" I called up to her, as I began scrambling to keep up. "Wait a second! You can't just imagine up a house for yourself like that! Even if you had the money, you'd have to plan it, and then spend a bunch of time working on it!"

She looked down at me through one torn elbow of her sweatshirt.

"Not if you're a finder," she said.

★　★　★

So we climbed and climbed, she leading, me trying to keep up. Finally, my legs were absolutely about to drop off.

"Stuhhh," I wheezed up to Vern. "Stuuhh . . . Stop!"

She stopped, turned around, and moved over to a little overhang of rock. She sat there, smiling her usual half-smile down at me. I dragged up there, too, and plopped down beside her.

"Whuh," I said, letting my poor body let go. I dropped back to a semi-lying-down position, propped up on my elbows.

"You're doing good," she said. "If I was your coach, like we talked about, I'd be proud."

"Thanks," I said, when I had enough breath. "If my metabolism wasn't so crummy, maybe I'd try this more often."

Vern stared across the hills.

"Why do you think your metabolism's crummy?" she asked without looking at me.

"Because my mother's is," I answered. "And I'm just like her, always have been."

Vern turned to look at me through her long, blowing bangs. "You're not her, though," she said.

I shrugged, thinking that was pretty obvious. I craned my neck around, sure that the summit of Hackberry Slope must be right above us by now, a few hundred feet. But to my surprise it looked as far away as ever.

"Listen, how do we know your supposed house is on this side of the slope?" I asked. I hoped to move the conversation around to the point where I could suggest starting back down. "Really, it could be anywhere, not necessarily just up closer to the top. Maybe we should just give . . ."

"Yes."

She slammed one fist into the other hand and said the word with all the power and impressive authority of someone who really knew what they were talking about. Then her eyes suddenly fuzzed over, like she was a light year or two away. She brought that key to her teeth and began clicking. I'd figured she couldn't keep from it forever.

"Oh, Lorelei, yes. You're right," she whispered. Click, click, click. "I can feel it now, calling to me from the other side of the mountain. Come on!"

And she jumped to her feet, began scrambling through the brush to blaze a trail. At least we were moving horizontally then, which is a lot easier than moving upward vertically. I pictured the two of us, gnomelike, dragging that trail behind us as if we were trying to fasten a belt around the huge, ancient mountain.

★　★　★

After about another hour we'd moved from the shady side of the slope into the sun. I was actually sweating inside the thick down of my jacket, though I could tell from the ice crystals on the cedars that it was still below freezing. We stopped to rest for a minute, sat on a big rock jutting from the trail. I took off my coat.

"Want to wear this a while?" I asked Vern. I'd been kind of wondering if she was warm enough in that holey sweatshirt.

She shrugged, reached out, and touched the collar.

"Nah. I might wreck it," she said. "I'm hard on clothes."

A picture of her that first morning—could it be just last Monday?—flashed through my head. That skimpy T-shirt, that too-short, too-tight skirt. She'd reminded me of a boy, the way she sat hunched that morning, caving in her chest and acting like she had more inches of legs than she knew what to do with.

Now I looked at her, trying to figure out if she really was like a boy, or a tomboy, or something.

No. Her clothes were just too tight. Under them, what there was of them, she had a great body. The body of an athlete. A girl athlete.

"You know, you look much more like a Vernita than a Vern," I said, thinking out loud.

She turned and looked at me, quickly, suspiciously—like she thought I was making a joke. When she saw I wasn't she seemed sort of shocked.

"Really?" she said.

"Yeah. I'd give practically anything to have a body like yours. You just seem kind of, I don't know . . . ashamed of it or something. I wouldn't be."

"I bet you've lost a pound or two already today," Vern murmured, sitting up a little straighter and staring down at her chest.

"Nah," I said back, quickly. I've never been able to stand the thought of anyone looking closely at me, and though Vern was inspecting herself at the moment, I was afraid she'd look at me next, as a comparison or to be polite or something. So I slipped back into my jacket to hide the worst of my blubber, just in case.

But I decided even if Vern talked about my fat I wouldn't mention my metabolism again, wouldn't use it as an excuse. I guessed what Vern had told me earlier was possible, when you thought about it. I loved my mom a lot, but I wasn't, after all, just exactly like her.

As far as I knew, for instance, she had never owned a single fish in her life.

Chapter 15

The sun went out over the mountain, making the sunny side the shady side. It was afternoon. My legs had long since passed the point of being tired and yowling to me with pain every inch of the way. They had decided to just shut up and put up with things. I guess they knew they could never find their way down now, without Vern. And she was on the trail of her house. For the last half hour she'd turned into a regular bloodhound, hiking hunkered down and stealthy. Alert to each sound, each shadow. A triple tornado obviously couldn't have pulled her from that mountain by then. I doubted if she'd even notice one.

"You know, school will be over for the day before long I'll bet," I suggested, meekly, at one point. "I'd better be thinking about getting home, at least before dark."

"Shhh!" she hissed back at me, then listened to the still air again, sniffed it.

Sniffed it! Exactly like a bloodhound.

I sighed, shook my head, and followed her, quietly.

★　★　★

And then, suddenly, she stopped. I nearly ran into her back.

"What?" I whispered. I looked around, but only saw tall cedars blending back into shadows on one side of us, a few feet of rocky ground falling away sharply on the other.

She turned around, faced me solemnly.

"Lorelei, what were you saying when I first saw you this morning?"

I pretended not to understand. I'm not that wild about everybody knowing about the contests I do with myself.

"Huh? Saying?"

"You said, 'I, Lori Sumner, have come in search of Vernita Hittlinger,'" she quoted, perfectly. "'If I don't see any trace of her in the next minute and a half I'll take that as a sign I'm not meant to ever.'"

"Why'd you ask what I was saying if you knew?" I muttered, flustered and perturbed.

"But did you mean just 'not meant to ever' like not meant to ever find her? Or did you mean 'not meant to ever . . .' something else? 'Cause it seems kind of like you would have said 'not ever meant to' if that's all you meant, instead of 'not meant to ever.' Know what I mean?"

"What difference does it make?!" I exploded. "Let's get on with this hike, okay? 'Cause my mother's going to kill me when I get home as it is!"

She nodded, like that made sense, and turned back around. She looked up the trail ahead of us, if you could call the tangle of weeds we were whacking through a trail.

"I think we're almost there," she whispered.

And we were. Around the next sharp, jutting curve was Vernita's house.

*   *   *

It was set deep in a nook of poplars, nearly covered with brown, frozen ivy vines and the roof loaded full of barnswallow nests. It wasn't exactly a Victorian mansion—more like somebody's old broken-down hunting cabin. One story, with a big sagging porch running all along the front. There was one green rubber boot sitting on the porch, along with a rain barrel and a gob of beer cans. Most of the windows were either broken out or had never had glass to begin with.

Vernita was entranced. She just stood there, her mouth partway open, rubbing her key.

"I knew it," she finally breathed, so low I hardly heard. "Come on, let's go in."

I grabbed her elbow, alarm sliding through me.

"Vern, wait!"

She turned to me, puzzled and frowning, that dazed and dreamy look still in her eyes.

"Uh, Vern? What do you think we'll find inside?"

She shrugged. "Furniture. Curtains. House things."

Anyone but Vern could have seen at a glance that a

house with no windows and all those barnswallow nests on the roof would be a filthy disaster inside. I wanted to protect her from ever seeing that, but I knew that was hopeless. So I just tried to soften the coming blow.

"Listen, it's probably been deserted for a long time. Just don't get your hopes up, okay?"

She laughed a little, humoring me. "Yeah, yeah. All right, already, Lorelei."

And then she ran through the high weeds, jumped the three broken steps, and was swallowed up by her house.

I didn't follow her inside, but I moved up to stand at the edge of the steps. Through the hole where the door had once been I could see the bonelike, rotten studs of walls with no plaster. I could see a big shaft of weak sunlight pouring through where a big chunk of the ceiling must have been missing. I could see part of one broken wooden chair, and no other furniture.

She was in there for quite a while. I sat down on one of the broken steps, waiting, then thought better of that when it started to cave in. I moved over and sat on a log in the jungly yard.

When she came out she moved slowly, but her face had no expression that I could read at all. She walked robotlike, one foot and then the other, over to sit beside me.

She put her hands in her lap, holding the key tightly, and just stared back at the house for a long time before she spoke. What she finally said was about the saddest thing I'd ever heard.

"I don't know, Lorelei. It needs some fixing up. I doubt if we can live there."

I took a deep breath and let it out. I kept trying to think of something to say, but there just wasn't anything. I put my hand on her shoulder.

"Vern," I finally forced out, my voice husky, "you're probably going then, right? To St. Louis? And, well, I feel like I know you better than anybody in some ways, but I don't understand a bunch of stuff about you at all. And now it looks like I never will. And that makes me feel so rotten."

I didn't know if that made sense, but Vern turned from her house to look me in the eye.

"It's a long story," she said, her voice small. "Us. My family. We're a long story."

I slid off the log to lie on the leaf-covered ground, my arms folded under my head. The late-afternoon sun poured down to cover my face like a warm mask.

"I'm too pooped to budge till I rest awhile anyway," I said. "So will you tell it? Your story?"

She sighed, and put her elbows on her knees and her chin in her hands. For a long time she just sat there, still and thin as the afternoon shadows. Then she spoke, quietly, toward the house.

"It's not like we've always lived in the station wagon," she began.

Chapter 16

∿ It's not like we've always lived in the station wagon.

When I was real little we lived in Washington, D.C., which as you probably know is the nation's capital. I can't remember our apartment there too well—I was only seven when we left Washington. I know we had furniture rented from a place called Friendly-Rents-It. I know that because when Daddy came home mad one night and said he was quitting his dead-end job at the box factory, Tyrone asked Mama later what "dead-end" meant. And she said, "It means we'll never be able to own the TV or refrigerator or couch that we rent from Friendly-Rents-It, honey."

The three weeks after Daddy quit that Washington job were the best three weeks of my life. We went to the Smoky Mountains and camped, while Daddy looked in that part of the country for new work. I just loved the mountains. I hadn't seen a real one since, until we came to Greenpoint.

But there weren't any jobs in the Smokies so we gave up on the East then and decided to try St. Louis. That's where Mama's sister, Aunt Thalia, lives. Her husband, Uncle Harper, told Daddy there might be openings soon at the car plant. Sure enough, Daddy got his longest job ever helping build cars there in St. Louis.

For all our four years in St. Louis we lived in Holiday Gardens Mobile Home Village in a long, green trailer. You could ride a bike from there to the Mississippi River and the Gateway Arch.

The trailer and its furniture were owned by Aunt Thalia and Uncle Harper, but we paid them rent for it, and I had my own room with the rug on the floor that I got in the Smoky Mountains. We each got to buy one souvenir, and the rug was mine. It was deep white plush with a black bear in the middle. I named him Herman and tried to hit his middle with my feet in the morning. I hated to step right on his head, though sometimes I missed and did.

When the car plant in St. Louis closed down is when we started living in the station wagon. I was eleven then and just out of fifth grade. Aunt Thalia said we were welcome to stay in the trailer till Daddy found another job and we got back on our feet, so we did for a couple of weeks. Then one night Daddy threw three beer bottles through the big picture window above the couch. Well, actually he threw two bottles through the window and one through the TV set. Maybe it was losing the TV set that made Uncle

Harper the most mad, though it wasn't really working anyway, which is partly why Daddy threw the bottles, I think.

Anyway, Daddy had been considering for a while moving on to Kansas City, so he said Uncle Harper kicking us out was a blessing in disguise. Mama worked for a few hours each week running the dry cleaning machine in a big laundromat near us, and the women who worked with her kept talking about all the wonderful jobs in Kansas City. They said all the good jobs in the whole state were going begging in Kansas City, while St. Louis suffered with the car plant closing and a bunch of other bad stuff like that happening. Daddy said that sounded just about right to him.

So the morning after Daddy threw the bottles and he and Uncle Harper got in their yelling fight, we took off for Kansas City in the station wagon. Mom said pack one suitcase apiece. Aunt Thalia came into my room in the trailer, I remember, while I was packing. She just stood there in my doorway, looking at me. Her arms were crossed, and she kept moving one hand up and down across the other arm. She kept chewing on her lip, too. I could tell she was sad, so I tried to think of a joke or something to cheer her up.

"Will you take care of Herman for me?" I finally asked. "Just be careful not to step on his head, specially when he's hungry."

She didn't laugh. So I did, hoping she'd realize that was a joke and feel a little better. I have a horrible laugh now, though, as you've possibly noticed.

And it was starting to get disgusting even then. It's kind of like my voice keeps changing or something, getting lower and lower like a boy's. My laughs sound like frog croaks.

Anyway, Aunt Thalia didn't laugh along, didn't even smile. She just looked a little sadder. I thought that might be partly because my laugh was so nauseating, but she moved close to me and took both my arms in her hands.

"Vernita, why don't you take Herman with you?" she asked. Her voice was the opposite of mine—always very soft, very quiet. I couldn't hear her half of the time and was always having to ask her to repeat herself. Mom talks like that, too, I guess because they're sisters.

"No room in the car," I said.

Aunt Thalia didn't answer that. She just opened her mouth, then closed it again and dropped her hands from my arms. I went on packing, then sat on my suitcase there on the bed, forcing it shut.

Now, though, I wish I had taken Herman. I could have just spread him across the floor in the back of the station wagon, where I've ended up sleeping most of the last year and three months. He would have been good company, plus he would have made it softer on top of the big crack in the floor where the door to the tire compartment is.

But that morning we left, I remember, I was way too scared of Daddy's bad mood to ask him about anything, especially anything as insignificant as taking a bear rug along in the car with us. Besides, how could

I have known how long I'd be sleeping in the back like that?

How could anybody know?

★ ★ ★

We left St. Louis on July 24. My brother Tyrone kept pouting because it was just six days till his eighth birthday and Daddy had sort of promised him he could go to a Cardinals game for it.

"Maybe we'll take you to see the Royals," Mom said over her shoulder as we took off down Highway 70 that day. "Maybe we'll even see George Brett play, how's that?"

Although I was concentrating hard on seeing the Arch for the last time, I couldn't help thinking how even Mom with her limited sports knowledge should have known better than to tempt a dyed-in-the-wool Cards fan with a Royals game.

"I'd rather eat worms," Tyrone said.

And then there it was—the Arch. Rising from the buildings on one side of it and the river on the other like a shining rainbow from space.

I've sometimes wondered, Lorelei—do I love the sky because I grew up for nearly four years in the city with the Arch, or do I love the Arch because I just naturally love the sky?

Anyway, I know I really love the Arch because watching it out the back window of our 1976 Oldsmobile that day till it was just a dazzle at the tops of the downtown buildings—well, I'm embarrassed to admit it, but that made me cry, in spite of my determination not to let moving get to me.

99

But when the Arch was completely out of view and I lay down on the floor there in the back of the station wagon, I noticed that the sky is kind of like a ceiling or something. Kind of like part of a house that never ends, so you're always sort of at home.

When I figured that out, I started to feel a little better.

★   ★   ★

It was hard finding a campground when we arrived in Kansas City. We drove around and around for hours it seemed like, and finally we came to this big huge place called Swope Park. It was kind of like Forest Park in St. Louis—full of things for people to do, like a zoo and an outdoor theater and stuff. There were gobs of trees and trash cans and picnic tables, but it didn't exactly look like they wanted people spending the night there. I didn't see any tents or anything like that.

Still, when Daddy pulled the car under a tree and started unloading our junk, I figured we were there to stay, at least till he could latch on to one of the millions of good jobs we'd heard about.

The next morning, he took off in the Oldsmobile, and Mom, Tyrone, and I settled into a pattern of sitting around the park, waiting for night when he might come home with some good news.

We did that every day that first week in Kansas City. The zoo was only about two blocks down from us, and Tyrone kept wanting to go over there. But Mom had decided that would be his birthday treat, so she wouldn't let him jump the gun.

"But it won't be a real treat anyway, because I'll

be too worn out from pestering about it to enjoy it," Tyrone pointed out the morning before his birthday.

That day was even hotter and more humid than the four before it had been. Everytime I thought about the boring hours of sweating and waiting, something in me wanted to explode.

"So quit pestering," I told Tyrone.

He seemed to think about that, and then shrugged and accepted it, and ran to the swings down the hill.

Mom pushed her light brown hair back from her face, then lifted it and fanned her neck with her hand.

"Thanks for handling that, Vernita," she said softly. "I feel so . . . drained today."

I got up from the bench of the picnic table and moved over to sit in the grass and lean against an elm tree. I wanted a better look at my mother, because I was starting to be worried about her.

Her dress had passed the fresh-looking stage the day before, and now it looked pretty grungy. The back had been sticking to her, then drying, then sticking to her for three days. It's okay for a kid to sweat and dry and sweat some more, but I don't think mothers handle that kind of thing too well. Mine wasn't, anyway—I could tell that from the dark circles appearing under her gray eyes. She's pretty delicate. She and Aunt Thalia both are kind of more like shadows than real people. They sort of drift around, picking up things for people. Picking up things their kids leave out, or their husbands throw, or everybody just drops.

"I kind of think we should check into a motel to get out of this heat," I told her that day.

She smiled. "You that hot?" she asked, still fanning with her hand.

"Not me. You," I said. "You look all washed out."

But now that she mentioned it, I was plenty hot, too. Burning up, just sitting there in that stupid humid park with nothing to do.

She dropped her hair back down, put a hand up to shield her eyes from the sun, and searched the playground in the distance for Tyrone.

"Oh, I'm fine," she said. "Just fine. And we need to save what little money we've got."

Well, I'd seen my Dad open his billfold at a gas station the night before. And there had been twenty-dollar bills there. I'd seen them. Maybe Mom hadn't, but I had.

"But we're loaded!" I told her. "We can afford to splurge, and besides, we should celebrate because Daddy will have a good job soon."

I started thinking about the Capri Court Motor Lodge we'd passed on the way into Kansas City four days before. I just couldn't get it out of my head. It had a kidney-shaped swimming pool in front, and lots of kids were jumping off the edges of it.

"Come on, Mom. Please? Let's ask Daddy when he comes back tonight. I know he'll go along. Please?"

Back then, I thought all you had to do to get a grown-up to do something was nag them long enough. It didn't occur to me to figure out if something was possible. I guess I thought anything was easy for grown-ups.

I know better now, of course. There are gobs of things in life that aren't easy or maybe even possible, for grown-ups or anybody else, Lorelei. Have you noticed?

Fifteen months of living mostly in a station wagon teaches you stuff like that.

Chapter 17

I can't remember what Mom answered to that big plea I made to stay in the Capri Court Motor Lodge. Whatever she said, it turned out not to matter. Because when Daddy got home that night, he was in a rotten mood, and none of us had the nerve to even talk to him, let alone to ask him about a motel.

Mom quickly and quietly cooked one of our usual simple camp suppers on the park grill, and then I went with Tyrone back to the playground so Mom and Daddy could have some time alone, and she could settle him down.

It was tagging along with Tyrone to all those playgrounds for a year and three months that got me into doing gymnastics. At first I just sort of twirled around on the low bars, but then I got bored with that and started swinging on the hanging rings, when whatever campground or park we were in had them. Sometimes there was a climbing rope, sometimes not.

Once, we parked for two weeks near a forest in Oklahoma, and I found some grape vines that were strong enough to take my weight and climbed and climbed for all I was worth.

That was great.

Anyway, Tyrone and I spent the hours between supper and dark at the playground that night before Tyrone's birthday. We could hear our father's voice loud and frustrated most of that time. We could sometimes hear our mother's voice, gentle and comforting but sad and tired. When we got a little scared alone in the dark, we went back up the hill and got into the car. Tyrone got into his He-Man sleeping bag in the backseat and I got in my usual place by the big window in the rear section. We pretended to go right to sleep. Tyrone even started in with some fake snores.

But really, it would have been pretty hard for anybody to sleep with the kind of nerve-wracking conversation our parents were having going on mere yards away.

I stared out at the stars and wondered if those ladies in the laundromat in St. Louis had known what they were talking about. It was beginning to look to me like Kansas City was every bit as hard up for good jobs as St. Louis was.

★ ★ ★

It seemed like it took me forever to get to sleep that night. And when I finally did drift off, the next thing I knew there was a real bright light shining into the back window of the station wagon. I stuck my head out from under my blanket and saw my dad standing shirtless, scratching his messy hair, talking to a policeman over near the trash can.

"I understand that, sir. But you folks have nevertheless got to move along now," I heard the policeman saying. "This area is equipped for daytime use only."

The light on the policeman's car was turning and flashing. When it turned in the right direction, I could see my mother, quickly stacking things beside the car and deflating the inflatable mattress she and Daddy had been sleeping on on top of the picnic table.

She quietly opened Tyrone's door and pushed his feet up farther on the backseat, then started loading stuff beside him.

"Mom?" I asked groggily.

"Shhh," she said, moving quickly and efficiently in the darkness. "Don't wake your brother."

I squinted, trying to see her face. When the light flashed in our direction, I saw she had no expression, but her skin looked pulled tight across her cheeks and forehead.

The policeman and my father were still talking. My father was waving his arms around but he wasn't yelling, which was a relief. The policeman looked young and nice, and embarrassed. He had his ticket book in his hand, but he wasn't writing in it. He just kept flapping the cover open and closed, looking at the ground and shaking his head.

I swallowed, feeling embarrassed, too.

"Fold these, Vern," Mom whispered, stuffing some

106

blankets and the tablecloth from the picnic table back toward me.

I obeyed, glad to have something to do.

Then, finally, my father came to the car and slid in under the steering wheel. He just sat there while the policeman got back into his patrol car and drove silently back onto the main park road.

"Jack?" Mom had finished packing us up, and quickly got into her own place in front. She put a hand on the back of Daddy's seat, but didn't dare touch him.

Daddy gripped the wheel with both hands, then lowered his forehead onto them. He breathed in and out, in and out. Then he sat back up straight.

"A shelter, Wanda," he said in a hollow, scary way. "For the homeless. Can you believe that? He gave me the address of a local shelter for the homeless. Like we were some kind of lowlifes or something that needed a handout."

"Oh, Jack," Mama repeated softly, then touched his shoulder. "Maybe just for the rest of the night. What harm?"

I slunk deep into my blankets, covered my head. A couple of minutes later, Daddy started the car, and we drove fast and hard out of Swope Park, our tires squealing.

★　★　★

I'm not sure because I finally fell deep asleep, but it seems like Daddy drove around and around the rest of that night. When I woke up it was bright outside, Mom was driving the Oldsmobile, and Daddy was nowhere to be seen. Tyrone was still asleep.

107

There were the kind of fast-food places and car re-pair shops on each side of the road that you see in the suburbs.

"Where are we?" I asked Mom, totally discom-bobulated. I lunged up, hooked my elbows over the front seat and my feet over the back, and hung like a bridge, my T-shirt tail swishing down onto Tyrone's head. "Where's Daddy?"

"Well, I think we're about in Raytown right now, or maybe Independence," Mom whispered to me. "I have trouble keeping places straight around here. I left Daddy at the big employment office downtown an hour or so ago. He said we should keep the car today, to go to the zoo for Ronie's birthday."

"Murrphh," growled Tyrone, batting at my shirt.

I unhooked one arm from the seat and tucked my shirt into my pajama bottoms.

"Where will we stay tonight?" I asked.

Mom didn't answer for a long time. Tyrone punched and kicked at me in his sleep, and I retreated back to my own section and started rummaging around for my socks in the blankets and hastily loaded cooking junk.

"Somewhere," I heard Mom say quietly then.

Chapter 18

We had to make one detour on our way to the zoo. We had to go back to our illegal campsite in Swope Park to look for Tyrone's Cardinals hat.

He discovered it was missing the second he woke up. It was kind of like he just opened his eyes and noticed immediately his head was lighter or something.

"Happy birthday, Ronie!" I called over the seat to him when I saw his feet kicking off his sleeping bag.

"Happy birthday, son!" Mom echoed, beaming toward him in the rearview mirror.

I think both Mom and I were acting super cheerful so Tyrone would have a good day, in spite of everything being kind of a mess at the moment.

But you could tell something was wrong from the way the sleeping bag was jerking wildly in the air. And a few seconds later, Tyrone popped up onto his knees on his seat, throwing blankets and clothes and stuff around like a red-haired, frantic tornado.

"Okay, who stole it?" he demanded, turning angrily from me to Mom, and back to me again. Then I guess he figured out that that was pretty far-fetched, and the anger in his voice quickly became a kind of panicky sadness. He also changed his question. "Where's my hat, Mom? It's gone! My Cards hat is gone!"

"Oh, no," Mom said. Then she stopped the car and slid from under the wheel to stretch over and help Tyrone search through the junk on his seat. "Well, don't worry. It couldn't have just got up and walked away," she said.

Why do grown-ups say silly, obvious stuff like that? A big truck with "K.C. Supply" printed on the door squeezed past us and honked. I guess we were stopped kind of in a traffic lane. Mom looked nervously out the window, her mouth a tight line that was supposed to be a sort of apologetic smile but looked more like a wince.

"I bet it's at the playground by where we camped," I said, after glowering at the rude truckdriver and making a mental note never to shop at K.C. Supply, no matter how rich we got when Daddy got this great Kansas City job and no matter how much they begged for our business. "Let's go back there and look."

Mom seemed nearly limp with relief at my suggestion. "Oh, yes, that's surely where it is!" she said, bouncing back around into her seat to put the car in gear.

"Promise?" said Tyrone, and his eyes looked like they were rimmed in red marker. "Vern, you promise it's at the playground?"

"Oh, Tyrone . . ." I began, hoping to explain about things you can promise and things you can't.

But by then his chest was moving up and down real quick, like a bird's.

"Oh, okay. Promise," I said quickly.

*   *   *

We all looked for a long time, but it wasn't there. My theory is that it was left there, but stolen. Well, not exactly stolen. Just picked up by some kid who thought the original owner probably wasn't coming back.

Tyrone was practically stiff with grief. He wouldn't talk, wouldn't bend at the knees. Just sat there in the backseat with his legs straight out, staring numbly at the raggedy laces in his tennis shoes.

"Oh, honey. Maybe they have hats at the zoo," Mom said hopefully. She pulled the car slowly from the place we'd left in such a hurry the night before. You could see our deep tracks in the mud by the drinking fountain.

I didn't think the zoo probably would have Cards hats. The gift stands in the two zoos I'd been in (the big one in St. Louis and a little roadside zoo outside of Peoria, Illinois) had stuff like plastic animals and sacks of prairie dog food. But nothing like hats. Evidently Tyrone didn't hold much hope for that, either. He didn't perk up a bit, just kept staring listlessly at his shoes like the world had fallen down to pieces around his feet.

*   *   *

Mom parked in the zoo lot, and we made our way to the entrance. There were about ten million people there. The people going in looked pretty cool and

111

happy. The ones coming out looked hot and miserable, though it wasn't even noon yet. A lady coming out the exit with her little girl in a stroller kept banging the stroller against the gate, yelling at it to open. Finally a man opened it and held it for them, I was relieved to see. The little girl rubbed her eyes, whining gently.

"Well, isn't this wonderful?" Mom asked, when we finally got inside the gates. She took a wadded up Kentucky Fried Chicken napkin from her purse and wiped her neck with it. "Where first? The elephants? Monkeys?"

I could see it was going to be a long, hard day. Mom was trying her best to make this into a celebration, but Tyrone was lost in a deep, pouty funk. I felt sorry for him, and at the same time I felt like shaking him till his eyes jiggled in their sockets. Couldn't he see how hard Mom was trying to get us to have fun?

"How about the zebras?" I suggested brightly, nudging Tyrone. "You love zebras, right? Don't you, still?"

He shrugged, stuck out his bottom lip, and started bouncing his heel on a big rock that was poking out of the dirt.

Mom sighed, and walked over and sat down on a bench in a little tangle of shade by the "desert mammals" exhibit. She leaned against the animal food dispenser, finally even resting her head on it.

"Aren't you ashamed, Ronie?" I hissed to my brother. "Don't you think she's beat, after driving around and around and around all night? Don't you think she's worried sick about Daddy and his job? And you can't even be nice and smile and stuff!"

He quit bouncing his heel and kicked, hard, at the buried rock. Then he turned on me.

"You promised, Vern," he spat out, tears standing hot in his eyes. "You promised."

I knew that was going to come up sooner or later. Suddenly, I didn't want to look Tyrone in the eye. There was a bunch of stuff he needed to learn about, but I didn't understand it yet enough to be the teacher. Maybe I never would understand it. How could I know?

All I knew was that promises don't always get kept, like when people lose jobs and can't get new ones and stuff. Life holds out lots of bright promises, but not all of them come true. I knew that much.

"I shouldn't have promised you'd find your hat, Tyrone," I admitted to him softly. "I just couldn't stand to see you cry, so I promised. But listen— there's still hope, you know."

For the first time that morning, he perked up. He quit kicking at that rock, and looked at me, something shining a little in his eyes.

"There is?" he asked.

"Sure," I answered. "Like Mom said, it's possible they have Cards hats here. Or maybe someplace else."

I didn't think I was offering an awful lot of new information, but I've noticed it's kind of hard to tell what will make someone decide to quit being grouchy and get happy.

Tyrone frowned hard, like he was thinking. Then he nodded, and I could tell he'd accepted the situation.

"Okay," he said. "Then let's go see those zebras."

It was about a thousand miles clear around to where the zebras were kept. They had safari buses you could ride for fifty cents, and if we'd known how far it was going to be we probably would have ridden one.

But we didn't know, so we just kept trudging and trudging through the dusty heat.

We passed the elephants. They looked awfully dry, and I wondered if they were suffering with the heat. I've wondered that before—does someone with a large body feel more pain, or cold, or other stuff like that than a person with a small body feels? One of the elephants kept shuffling side to side, side to side, like he was trying to take his mind off the temperature.

Then we passed the rhinos and the hippos. The hippos had a small pool and looked totally content submerged with their fat noses sticking out of the water like mounds of clay. One surfaced and sprayed water out his nose. Mom and I jumped back, but Tyrone stepped forward to get soaked.

And then, in the distance, we saw the zebras, grazing behind a high chain-link fence.

Since he was tiny, Tyrone has loved zebras. He has a collection of them—some stuffed, most plastic, one a kind of balloon thing you can use at the beach to float on, and one delicate blown glass on a key chain. His collection has been stored in St. Louis since we left. Aunt Thalia said she'd take good care of it for him, like she's taking care of my bear rug and a couple of other valuable things for me.

When Tyrone caught sight of the zebras grazing down the road from us, he set out toward them at a run. Mom and I looked at each other and smiled, wondering how he got that burst of energy. I was about to collapse, and she looked like she was, too. Boy, it was hot. Sweat trickled cold down my back and soaked the waistband of my shorts.

And then a strange thing happened.

As Mom and I watched, most of the zebras ran away, spooked by Tyrone charging up on them. They fled from the fence, deep into the foresty area where their water hole and sheds were set up.

But one stayed, and settled huge, dark eyes on Tyrone. It was a little one, not exactly a baby, but not a teenaged zebra yet, either. It looked like a zebra who had just turned eight people years, and it waited, calmly, for Tyrone to approach.

He walked up to the fence and stood nose to nose with the little zebra. They just looked at each other, the zebra chewing his grass slowly, Tyrone chewing his gum. Mom and I stopped. We didn't dare approach very near. I knew the little zebra would only stay for Tyrone. Don't ask me how I knew that, but I did, and evidently Mom did, too.

"Oh," she whispered, "wouldn't it be wonderful if that zebra would sprout wings, and Ty would jump on its back and they would fly away somewhere better?"

"Better?" I asked, turning to look at her. She had a funny look on her face, kind of like she was about to cry, something she hardly ever did.

She turned to look at me, and shrugged.

"Well, simpler," she said.

Then we sat in the grass together, and spent a long

time watching Tyrone and the zebra, until the zebra's mother came and got him and took him home.

★   ★   ★

We went to the monkey house then, but the monkeys were crabby, probably with the heat and the humidity, which was terrible in their closed-up building. One of the chimps kept hitting his friend on the head with a rubber ball bat, though his friend kept running away and stuck his poor head down between his legs, trying to hide.

Then we went to the reptile building. There were several crocodiles and alligators, which were very interesting. The biggest crocodile had a bunch of quarters and dimes on his back, and couldn't do a thing about getting them off. That worried me, and I bawled Tyrone out when he got ready to try and hit him with a nickel.

Finally, even Tyrone was pretty pooped. But to be sure we hadn't missed anything fabulously interesting, Mom suggested we spend a quarter apiece riding the zoo train around the center of the zoo.

And it was there, on the zoo train in Kansas City, that I first discovered I was a finder.

I was just relaxing, watching the jungly vines and trees and animal exhibits speed by, when something deep inside me told me to look at the ground.

"Look down, right at the gravel by the tracks, Vern," the tiny voice seemed to say. "There, you'll find something of value."

So I looked down, and three seconds hadn't passed before I saw it—a dollar bill, just lying there nearly within arm's reach of my seat on the train! I couldn't get it, of course, and we were quickly far past it. But it had been there, there was absolutely no doubt in the world about that.

I was stunned, and felt my blood pounding in my ears as I let the significance of what had just happened sink in.

I tried to share what I was feeling with Mom.

"But you couldn't reach it?" she asked when I'd finished, looking disappointed.

But that wasn't the point.

I think I realized even then, right from the first day of my being a finder, that everything that's found isn't necessarily to be kept.

It's the finding itself that's the amazing thing.

Chapter 19

⟨≈⟩**O**n the way out of the zoo we stopped in the gift shop. They didn't have Cards hats, or even Royals hats. But Tyrone got a little stuffed zebra, which he named Randy. Randy seemed to take the edge off Tyrone's hat disappointment.

Maybe I remember all the stuff that happened that day at the Kansas City Zoo so well because it was the last day we had that seemed normal.

Up till that day, it was just like we were camping, on a great adventure like that time in the Smoky Mountains. I was certain that any minute Daddy would get one of those great Kansas City jobs, and we would go house or trailer hunting, and things would settle down.

But when Mom and Tyrone and I drove up to the big Job Service building downtown, still hot and dusty from the zoo, things went downhill fast.

Mom parked the car by the building and told

Tyrone and me to wait while she went in to see if Daddy was around, or if he had been sent out to see about a job somewhere. But before she could even get out of the car, Daddy came lumbering out the big glass doors of the building, not looking cheerful. Not looking cheerful a bit.

My heart started pounding real hard, and I kept thinking over and over again—oh, please, let him wish Tyrone a happy birthday. Just let everything be okay and let him smile and wish Ronie a happy birthday.

Mom slid quickly to the passenger side of the front seat, her shoulders stiff like she was braced for something bad. Daddy threw himself under the wheel and slammed the door hard. He turned the key in the ignition, but it screeched because the car was already on. He jerked his head around to see if traffic was clear, then pulled from the curb so fast I fell over and smashed against Tyrone. He had Randy up against his face, sort of rubbing his ear with him.

We sailed through traffic like that, weaving, going fast. Daddy looked straight out the windshield, not talking. He stuck a cigarette into his mouth and punched the lighter hard, so hard it didn't stick in. He punched it a second time, then punched the metal of the dashboard above it.

"Jack," Mom whispered.

He didn't answer her, but he kind of slowed down a little bit.

"Honey?" she said. "No jobs today?"

"Or ever," he said hoarsely. "Or ever in this stinking place, or any other stinking, rotten place."

119

Kansas City didn't stink, even in the zoo, except for maybe the reptile house. Kansas City smelled good, like flowers and good cooking. And there were pretty fountains all over the place. I liked Kansas City. But I didn't tell Daddy that, of course. I just sat there in the backseat, petrified, hoping Tyrone was doing okay because he looked white as a sheet and it was his birthday and everything.

Finally, after a while of driving scary like that, Daddy pulled the car up in a parking lot behind a yellow brick building with torn green awnings.

"We're staying here tonight," he said. "Tomorrow we go on to where the real jobs are, down south."

He got out of the car, kicked his door shut, and began walking toward the building.

"Where are we?" I whispered to Mom.

She turned toward me, but she didn't answer right away. Her face was white, too, like Tyrone's. For the first time I noticed how much alike they looked, with their dark eyes that seemed so huge and easy to hurt.

I turned to Tyrone.

"Don't worry. He'll remember it's your birthday," I reassured him. "He just had a lousy day, that's all."

"Sure," Tyrone said, in a whisper. "I know."

★　　★　　★

We all got out of the car then and followed Daddy into the building, which turned out to be Haven House, the shelter for homeless people the policeman had told Daddy about the night before.

Everyone was very nice to us there, but I wanted to keep telling them that we didn't really belong there, that we were just passing through and were more like travelers or campers than homeless people.

They assigned us to a room with two beds in it, a fairly big one and a small cot, and we got the sleeping bags out of the car to use for bedding. Tyrone wanted to sleep in his He-Man bag on the floor in the corner, which left the cot for me.

We ate with a bunch of other people in this cafeteria kind of place they had right there in the shelter. We'd barely gotten our food down when Daddy got up from the table and we followed him upstairs to our room, and all silently turned in for the night.

Lying on that cot, I tried to remember if Daddy had said a single word to any of us that night, and couldn't remember that he had. I strained to hear, but didn't think he and Mom were talking in the bed on the other side of the room, either.

★　★　★

I woke up a while later. Normally I can pretty well tell nighttime by the way the moon and stars look, but there were no windows in this room at Haven House.

I hadn't been dreaming, and if the moon wasn't shining on my face, what had woken me up, then?

It was the sound of low voices, coming from the direction of Tyrone's sleeping corner. I held my breath, froze so no one would think I was awake, and listened.

". . . didn't want to act like that. Understand what I'm saying, son? It was just such a rotten, hard day. And I guess I wanted to be along for your birthday trip to the zoo. I did think of your birthday, all day.

Thought of how proud it makes me to have you so grown up and all. Believe me, son?"

"Sure, Dad. I missed you, though."

"Yeah. Me, too. I missed you."

A car went by fast outside, drowning out the low murmur of their voices. I frowned, and wished it past. Something that sounded like a big truck went by then, and after it was gone I could hear again.

". . . jobs for real men are farther south, toward the Gulf Coast. I should have thought of that right off. Jobs in oil, and in ranching. Maybe something will come along in Oklahoma, or if not, then for sure in Texas. It's gonna be all right, whichever way it goes. Whichever way. But I just can't stay here and work for darned peanuts. Not with rents like they are. You understand, boy? We've got to move along, toward our true dreams. It just won't do to stop now and struggle the rest of our days."

"No," Tyrone said softly, agreeing. "Dad? I lost my hat. It was stoled, I think."

Then there was silence for quite a while. I pictured my father and Tyrone, sharing that sleeping bag there in the total darkness across the room. Daddy's feet would be sticking out the bottom, and his arms would be folded behind his mass of shaggy dark hair. He would be staring at the ceiling, though he wouldn't be able to see it. Tyrone would be curled on his side, facing toward Daddy, Randy probably in the crook of his neck.

"I'll get you another hat, son." My father's voice sounded low and tired. "Shoot, I'll buy you a whole danged Cardinals outfit when we get to where we're goin'. Glove and all."

So the next morning we packed up and set out on Route I-35 across the state of Kansas. When we reached Wichita, early in the afternoon, we plunged straight south, aimed toward the state of Oklahoma like a Cherokee Indian arrow.

Chapter 20

⟍⟋**W**e stayed in Oklahoma City for the month of August, and the months of September and October. We bought a canvas tent at the Army surplus store, and set it up at a campground outside of the city. Mom and Daddy slept inside it each night, and Tyrone and I kept sleeping in the car.

Mom and Daddy both quickly found part-time jobs in Oklahoma City—Mom at a restaurant, and Daddy at an auto supply parts store. We expected that at any minute the Job Service people would call and tell Daddy there was a great full-time job open for him at one of the petroleum companies. Of course, it would have been hard for them to call, since we didn't have a phone. What I meant was, Daddy went in to check at Job Service three times a week, which was as often as you were supposed to. Mom explained that they got crabby if you went oftener.

I'd never seen red dirt like they had in Oklahoma.

Or brighter stars. That's when I got real interested in constellations, lying at night looking through the cracked glass in the back of the station wagon. I bought a book on them at a neat place called the Kirkpatrick Center, which had all kinds of science displays and stuff. It was across the road from the Oklahoma City Zoo, where we went a couple of times. Both the zoo and the science center were real cheap for kids, and Tyrone loved them. He made friends with the zebras in Oklahoma City, too.

The constellation book was kind of expensive— $5.95. But Mom said it would be worth it if I could learn some stuff that I could use later in science classes.

When she said that, it was late August and for the first time I really thought about the fact that school would soon be starting. Something in her tone of voice reminded me of it.

"I guess you and Tyrone should be enrolled somewhere," she said then, sounding exhausted. She'd been working twelve hours that day. That's kind of how her shifts at the restaurant went. Twelve hours on, then a couple of days off. On her off days, she and Tyrone and I went around looking for cheap apartments or trailers. The trouble was, everybody wanted two months' rent in advance, and that amounted to about a million dollars or so.

"Maybe we should just wait till we're really settled," I suggested. "To enroll in school, I mean. It's gonna be kind of tricky doing it this way."

I suddenly felt like this whole conversation was taking place inside a nightmare I was having. I was starting to realize I hadn't thought about school starting because I just couldn't handle thinking about it. Could we really be expected to go to school while we were still sleeping in the car, washing up every couple of days at the park rest rooms, and cooking most of our meals over a campfire?

Mom put her elbows on the picnic table where we were sitting, and put her face in her hands. She had her hair in a tight bun like the restaurant required, and she was still wearing her light green waitress outfit. It was getting dark. Daddy was still at work, and Tyrone was down the hill throwing rocks at frogs near the creek.

"I don't know. I just don't know," she whispered, shaking her head with her face still covered like that. "I think the law requires kids to be in school in September. Oh, I just don't know what to do about this."

I could tell she was pretty upset, but I wasn't feeling too hot myself. All of a sudden my head was filling with gruesome pictures of myself and Tyrone trying to blend in with a bunch of strangers when I didn't have a shower or a big mirror or any of that stuff that I really needed to look good in the morning. And what if they asked our address? They'd ask that in class, wouldn't they? Make you fill out forms for lunch count and bus count and all that stuff? What would we give for an address—City Park?

"I'll be back," I murmured to Mom, and started to walk down the hill, toward Tyrone. I just needed to get away from this conversation, and I figured finding a gym set and working out on the flying rings would drive it from my head. But halfway down the hill I realized I could leave the conversation behind, but I couldn't ignore the basic problem any longer. It was locked in my head now, something I would have to face. There would come a day, soon, when I would have to walk up to some new school and actually enter it, dressed in one of the three wrinkled outfits I had crammed in my duffel bag.

So instead of going on down the hill, I went back to the car. I crawled into the space in the back that I'd begun to think of as my room. I stared out at the sky, which was just filling up with those bright, bright stars. The big crack in the window made a warped place in the sky. When you moved slightly it was like a sheet had been flipped in the wind, and the stars all rolled a little.

I lay there and nodded my head to see the stars move, till finally I managed to go to sleep.

★　★　★

We ended up starting that school year at Will Rogers Elementary School. Daddy handled things. Mom never did seem to be able to think about it.

I entered sixth grade, and Tyrone was enrolled in fourth.

We could have met the bus about two blocks away, at the corner of the campground where the houses started. But I talked Tyrone into walking to the next stop, about five blocks. That way, we didn't take a chance on anybody seeing us coming from the campground. They all just would figure we lived in one of the hundreds of trailers and one-story stucco houses crammed into that neighborhood.

Mom brought home stuff from the restaurant,

where she'd begun working a full-time shift, for our lunches. That was a relief because we didn't have to fill out lunch forms. But just when I thought the coast was clear, Miss Davis gave us health forms to fill out for the school nurse, and there was a huge space right at the top marked ADDRESS.

I thought hard and fast, and remembered the name of the street where we met the bus in the morning. "201 Elm Street," I wrote on the form. My heart thudded hard when Miss Davis collected those papers, and I was tense the rest of that day, wondering if the nurse would come and stand in the doorway and bellow that she wanted to talk to that lying address-thief, Vernita Hittlinger. But nothing like that happened.

It was about then that it occurred to me that probably every town in America had an Elm Street. I filed that information away, just in case I ever needed it again, which it turned out I certainly did.

★   ★   ★

I never did try for friends at Will Rogers. I had my hands full just keeping our school clothes rinsed out and the fire started for dinner at night and cooking water carried. In lots of ways, camping isn't fun but is more like plain old hard work. Mom looked tired to death when she finally got home each day, and Daddy was usually in a bad mood. I wanted to ask how much longer it was going to be till the good job with the petroleum firm started, but I didn't have the nerve. Not the way Daddy spent his evenings glowering into the fire like he wanted to tear everything around him to shreds.

Something was really starting to worry me, though.

It was beginning to get cold.

Did Daddy plan to camp like this all winter?

★   ★   ★

It was about the middle of October when Mom got sick, so sick she had to take a few days off work. One of those days was Saturday, which would usually have been a twelve-hour shift for her at the restaurant. I hardly ever had a chance to be with her anymore, so I decided I should take the opportunity to really pin her down on some things.

She had spent the morning sitting in the front seat of the car, wrapped in Tyrone's sleeping bag, resting her head back and coughing and wiping her nose every so often while she listened to the radio. I spent the morning at the gym set down the hill, working out and planning my strategy and trying to get rid of the butterflies that came into my stomach every time I thought about confronting Mom about our future.

When the questions I needed answered were finally organized in my mind, I went up the hill, opened the car door, and stuck my head in.

"Hi," I said cheerfully. "Mind some company?"

She smiled, looking pale and weak, and patted the seat beside her.

I quickly slid in under the wheel, grabbed it, and stared hard at the dust on the dashboard. Nervousness kept trying to sneak its way into me and make me chicken out on this conversation, but I kept pushing it back. I needed to get this straight.

"Okay," I said. "This is the thing. Are we just

going to stay in this place, like, forever? Like till we rot or freeze to death or something? Because I think we need a plan. I really do."

I stopped, swallowing. I didn't dare turn to meet her eyes. I just stared hard at the dust, waiting for her to agree or disagree.

But she didn't speak, just coughed a little.

"Okay then, one other thing," I went on, clearing my throat. "I have a two-part suggestion. First, we get a newspaper and start looking again for apartments. Second, we move into one."

There, I'd said it. It had been hard to get up the nerve, but somebody needed to take control of the situation, and my parents obviously had been too busy to realize you couldn't camp in winter!

But again, there was silence from my mother's side of the car. When I finally got up the nerve to turn to her, there were tears sliding down her cheeks, and her nose was running like a little kid's.

"Honey, I've spent my lunch hours looking for apartments for the past six weeks," she said, hiccuping a little. "Your father and I are both making minimum wage, and he's only being paid for twenty-five hours a week. And when I'm run-down and sick like this, I miss work and don't get paid at all. We can't do it, honey. We can't pay the deposits and such. Right now, for us, it's either buy food and car gas, or buy shelter. One or the other, not both."

I didn't know how I should react to this information.

It was certainly shocking, and disappointing.

But something far worse happened, that made the whole conversation go completely out of my head.

While I watched helplessly, Mom started coughing, hard and hoarse, and just couldn't stop. She couldn't get her breath for a real long time, and when the spell was finally over, she was so weak she just collapsed down on the seat and couldn't even talk.

I covered her up with every blanket and sleeping bag I could find, and tried to get hot tea down her, though she was too weak to drink it.

Luckily Daddy had ridden a bus to work that day, so I didn't have to worry about getting him picked up at the auto supply store. When he finally got back to the campsite he took one look at my mother, turned pale himself, and drove her to the emergency room of the nearest hospital.

They kept her there and put her in an oxygen tent.

She had double pneumonia, complicated by what they called complete physical exhaustion. The doctors said we were real lucky. She could have died.

Chapter 21

The night we left Mom at the hospital was the night I found the key.

Tyrone was so upset about leaving Mom that Dad had him sleep in the tent, with him. I tried for hours to get to sleep by myself in the car, but the stars out my window looked hard and sharp. They bored into my head, like the tire-compartment ridge underneath where I sleep always bores into my side.

So I snuck away from the campsite. I walked first down to the gym set, then followed the creek a little way into the scraggly woods at the edge of the campground. There were a bunch of beer cans lying in a heap. I left the path to go around them, and stepped on it. The key.

I knew for a certain fact that I was a finder by then, of course. I'd already found the gas cap Daddy left on top of the car that late night we got gas in Kansas, for instance. And I'd seen that dollar at the zoo, and found the car keys several times. And a bunch of other stuff.

But when I knelt there in those woods, heard a nightingale cry over the trickling water, and picked up that key, I knew that I had discovered the purpose of all my other finding. It was merely practice for this.

Finding this key, at this time, was a true sign that everything would be all right.

It was suddenly crystal clear to me that there was a house waiting for us somewhere, and that we only had to cut all these other problems out of the way, like people hacking through a dense jungle, to find it.

In fact, the key wasn't even an ordinary door key, not by a long shot. It was a gorgeous, fancy, antique iron key. And because of that I knew the house it was meant to open wouldn't be a trailer, or a little stucco shack, or even a regular suburban split-level like Aunt Thalia and Uncle Harper had.

The house my key would open to us would be a wonderful Victorian house, where we would have gardens and a real bathroom and everything. Where my mother could wear beautiful white gowns and rest on the veranda and never work a twelve-hour restaurant shift again. Where she and I could drink lemonade from crystal glasses without wondering if there were bugs in the bottom of them from being on the picnic table all night.

I practically ran back to the campsite with my key safe in my hand, and I had no more trouble getting to sleep that night. I knew instead of having nightmares about Mom coughing I'd have dreams about our house-to-be, and I couldn't wait to get started on them.

★ ★ ★

In a strange way, Mom getting sick like that really made things better for us for a while. I mean, I think we all realized what was important a little better, and when we moved the next day into the homeless shelter in downtown Oklahoma City, it wasn't such a big deal. Not nearly as big a deal as it had felt like that one night in Kansas City.

Daddy didn't even brood about it much. He was too busy worrying about Mom, and running back and forth between his job and the hospital.

It was when Mom was released, about two weeks later, that Daddy started brooding. Well, it wasn't really brooding. It was more like something in him changed, got quieter and gruffer and sadder. I think that was partly because we didn't have money for the hospital bill, and he had to fill out a bunch of forms and stuff and then the state paid it. And since Mom had lost her job and was too weak to work now anyway, money got to be real tight.

Real, real tight. Mom no longer even talked about getting a paper and looking for an apartment.

The afternoon Daddy finally had to go to the office where they give people welfare money, Mom told Tyrone and me not to even try to talk to him when he came back.

"He's a proud man, kids. He's used to having control," she said. "This asking for help from the government will be hard on him."

So we didn't stick around when he got home.

Instead, when we came home from school that day I stood watch by the window of our room in the shelter. At about 4:30 I saw our car drive up and stop in the parking lot. Daddy got out, glowering.

"Come on, Tyrone," I said quickly. "We got to get out of here so Mom can calm Daddy down."

And without a word of complaint Tyrone followed me out the back door, and around the corner, to where there was a smooth stretch of sidewalk by the side of the building.

I tried to teach Tyrone how to play jacks out there, while we waited for our parents to talk things out. The sidewalk was pretty cold—it was November by then—so we got some newspapers out of a trash can on the corner to sit on.

Tyrone was awful at jacks. Just awful. He kept throwing the ball too high, and sort of lunging at the jacks so they scattered worse instead of getting trapped in his hand. I tried to be patient, but my nerves were sort of shot anyway from wondering so hard what was going to happen to us. In the back of my mind, I pretty well knew that we'd reached some kind of turning point. I knew Daddy wouldn't just sit here and draw that welfare check each week. Something was going to happen, but what, I didn't know. I guess I was kind of hoping we would go back to St. Louis, where things hadn't been great, but had been better. Or maybe back to the Smoky Mountains, though I couldn't really see why we would have better luck there. I liked it there, though, a lot.

"I hate this stupid game!" Tyrone suddenly exploded, jumping to his feet and kicking my jacks in all directions.

I watched one of them roll closer and closer to the grate going down to the sewer below the sidewalk, and when it finally rolled in I knew I should feel furious with Tyrone. After all, it's not easy playing jacks with only nine jacks.

But when I looked up at him, ready to bawl him out, there was something about his face with all those freckles, and his poor bare head without its Cards cap holding down all his wild hair, and I just wanted to hug him instead of yelling at him. I couldn't, of course, because he would have punched me.

So instead, I stood up myself and dug in my jeans pocket till I found my key.

I held it out in the bright fall air between us.

"See this?" I said solemnly, hoping he'd realize the importance of what I was telling him. "This is our future, Ronie. Somewhere, I'm sure there's a house that this unlocks. Our house."

He just stood there, still panting with anger. But staring, round-eyed and impressed, at my key.

"Promise?" he finally whispered.

I sighed.

"Oh, Ronie, please. Let's don't get into that promise stuff again, okay?" I said.

After a minute he sighed and shrugged, and bent to start picking up the jacks.

★　　★　　★

When Tyrone and I had picked up nine of the jacks, we peered together into the grate, hoping the tenth one was still visible. Sure enough, it was lying on a sort of muddy ledge thing, down about two feet under the sidewalk.

Tyrone took out his gum, stuck it on a stick that was there in the street, and started trying to retrieve the lost jack. He was preoccupied that way and didn't see Mom when she came around the corner, a blanket around her thin shoulders like a shawl.

"Kids?" she said softly. "Come in. Your father and I need to talk with you."

I searched her face, my heart suddenly pounding.

"Don't worry, Vern. It'll be okay," she said, giving me a weak smile. "Your father has a plan."

★　★　★

The plan was to go to Texas.

We left the next morning.

At first I tried to keep track of the towns and cities in Texas where we camped while Daddy tried to break into either ranching or oil. The trouble was, it seemed like there were lots of people in Texas trying to do basically the same thing we were trying to do.

Still, it was warm. We could camp easily without risking Mom's health. We were there for most of a whole year.

We went to four schools, three in different parts of Houston and the other in a little town about twenty miles from San Antonio. I used "Elm Street" as an address all four times, and it worked.

Daddy had lots of jobs, and Mom worked some, too, when she started feeling good enough again. But they were the same kind of jobs they'd had in Oklahoma, clerking in stores or waitressing. They paid minimum wage, which Mom explained was pretty much next to nothing when it had to stretch to feed four people. A couple of times Daddy worked pumping gas.

I kept waiting for them to talk about looking for apartments, but I knew by now that you had to have about four or five hundred dollars together in one spot for that to happen. And since I couldn't picture us ever having half that much, I didn't hold my breath. Anyway, the longer we lived in the car the less real houses seemed. I mean, they seemed like far away things only other people could ever dream of having, like motorcycles and trips to Hawaii.

It scared me to feel like that. It scared me to start forgetting the smells and sounds and the feeling of a house.

So at a carnival in Laredo I spent the dollar Daddy gave me for rides on a neck chain and started keeping my key on it. And every night as I went to sleep I rubbed the key and pictured our Victorian house in my mind.

★   ★   ★

By the end of our second summer on the road, I was pretty much in the habit of living in the back of the car, watching the constellations whirl around me in the night, feeling for my key as I went to sleep.

I was also used to the crowded campgrounds and the flat, sandy promises of Texas. Every few days a new rumor would come around about a bunch of good jobs opening up. Those rumors would travel like electricity through all the people in all the cars and tents around us, and radios would be turned to loud, happy stations. You'd hear people laughing, and the smell of beer bought to celebrate would be strong in the muggy air.

And then, a day or two later, the rumor would turn out to be untrue, and jittery silence would settle back down on everybody. You'd only hear low, frustrated mumbling in the night air. That, and the sound of prairie birds and sad cowboy songs on the radios and little kids whining because it was hot.

That month we were in school in the little town of Bartleton outside of San Antonio, I heard some of the other kids talking about the campground where we were staying.

They called it a gypsy camp.

"My dad says those homeless people just live like bums out there," this one kid in my English class told his friend. "Like lazy gypsies in some filthy gypsy camp."

My eyes burned when I overheard that, but I didn't think there was any way they could know I was from that camp, and not from Elm Street. So I took a bunch of deep breaths, pulled a sheet of paper out of my spiral notebook, and started drawing a map of the constellations.

That calmed me down a lot, and I started drawing a map like that any time I needed to in school to make it through a class.

And when I got into my sleeping bag that night, and lay staring out at the stars, I thought about it and decided there was really nothing wrong with gypsies anyway. They were just basically misunderstood, as lots of people are.

Chapter 22

Then out of the blue Daddy came home one hot night the end of September and threw his Lonestar Fill-'er-Up cap down on the picnic table.

"River work," he announced loudly.

Mom eyed him for a second with a worried look in her eyes, but then started smiling when she saw he was in a good mood for a change.

"River work?" she asked quietly.

"Work on the river, woman!" he said, rushing over to where she was peeling potatoes and grabbing her into his arms. "A guy came by the filling station today on his way to Arkansas to work on the river, running canoe rides for the tourists. He stopped for a good thirty minutes, about talked my ear off. You could tell he could see I was a man hungry for an opportunity, and he sure enough had a hot tip for me. He says Arkansas is the new vacation wonderland for the entire Midwest, and the opportunities for work there are unlimited! Man's work, too—on the rivers, in the mountains! Not this pumping gas in the dusty sun, getting nowhere and having lots of company while you get there."

He ran his eyes around the crowded campground as he said that, then spat into the dirt. Mom hates it when he spits, but I guess she was too glad to have him enthused about something again to say anything.

Tyrone and I, meanwhile, huddled over by the fender of the car, watching. I had heard the word "mountains," and my heart was beating so fast I was worried it would bust through my chest and hop on down the road. But at the same time, it seemed too good to be true, so I tried not to let my hopes get as high as they were getting. I just held on to my key necklace, and tapped it against my teeth like I'd gotten in the habit of doing when I was nervous.

"Daddy?" Tyrone asked then, in a small voice that told me he was nervous, too. "Do you really think we're probably going someplace Randy will like?"

Daddy and Mom both looked at us then, and I saw tears in Mom's eyes. Maybe she was thinking the same thing I was, that it was kind of sad Tyrone didn't ask for promises anymore.

Daddy came and sat on the fender, put an arm around my waist, and took Tyrone on his knee.

"Kids, we're shaking this red Texas dust off our boots as soon as your mother and I can quit our jobs and draw our little pay," he said softly. "And we're moving up to northern Arkansas, where a man can be a man and make decent wages, and we can hold our heads high again."

141

So in October we traveled north, caught the edge of Oklahoma, and finally arrived here in the Boston Mountains of the Arkansas Ozarks. I'd never seen such a perfect place, at least not since the Smokies. In a way I realized I was being a little disloyal to the Arch, thinking like that. But your mountains pierce the very sky, Lorelei, and even the Arch can't do that. It was almost like they were whispering to me as we first drove through them—"Welcome home, Vern. Welcome home." I held on to my key as we zigged and zagged over the winding mountain roads, and tried not to want this as bad as I did.

★　★　★

We camped around for a couple of weeks late in October until our money was getting low, trying to figure out which of the towns would have the best river and mountain work prospects. Nothing jumped out at us, no great job landed in Daddy's lap. So we picked Greenpoint partly because there were three rivers near it, and lots of mountains. And partly because Mama and I thought the name sounded lucky.

I was thrilled to be settled here in the Jaycee Campground, but at the same time I knew what was coming and it gave me some sleepless nights.

School.

You never really get used to starting a new school. It's always scary, no matter how many times you do it. And starting Greenpoint Middle School scared me more than usual. When you get your hopes up, like I'd gotten my hopes up about settling here in spite of my determination not to, it changes everything.

142

Getting your hopes up is something you should abandon when you live in a station wagon, like ironed clothes and television. I knew that well by October. I just, unfortunately, forgot it.

★　★　★

So you know most of the rest of this stuff, Lorelei. Daddy let Tyrone and me off in front of the school last Monday, the first day of November. The secretary in the front office frowned and asked if we were enrolled, and I said my parents would be in soon to do that. Daddy always has us tell school people that, then if we stay around more than a week he comes in and enrolls us. He says there's no use wasting time on paperwork if we're not staying. Sometimes the school people go for that, sometimes they don't—depends on the place. Sometimes we have to spend the day in the office, till when Daddy or Mom comes to pick us up and gets trapped by the principal into filling out papers.

I guess my parents partly do things that way because they don't like to fake addresses any more than I do.

Anyway, at your school the secretary in the front office told us to go on to the gym, where everyone waited for the first hour bell to ring. I saw the little kids in the corner with bright plastic lunch boxes. They looked like they must have been the fifth-graders, so I gave Tyrone a tiny shove in that direction. I took off myself across the gym to where it looked like the sixth- and seventh-graders were sitting, in the bleachers.

Everything got quiet when I walked by. There was

some giggling. I expect that. That's how things always start. I try not to think about it too much, try not to wonder what about me is so funny.

I saw that spot where the bleachers make kind of a roof so people can't gawk at you very well, and made a beeline for it and sat down.

But I'd hardly had time to settle in there and take a deep breath when you came rushing up.

"Excuse me, but I believe this is my seat," you sort of wheezed at me.

Your arms were full of books, and your face was sort of jiggling like you were about to self-destruct.

I clicked my necklace on my teeth to block the sounds of giggling and whispering ringing in my ears. I hunched over, hoping to sink in my chest a little, which I knew was sticking out too much through Tyrone's T-shirt.

"Excuse me, but I always sit here!" you said again, sort of hysterically. No offense, Lorelei, but you were pretty hyper that morning. I wondered if you were going to faint or something.

I didn't know what to do, so I tried for a joke. "Don't see your name on it," I said.

But I'm sort of out of practice joking around with kids my age, and I was too petrified to say it right anyhow, so I don't think you got it.

"Please, I've been sitting here since sixth grade! Can't you scoot over?" you pleaded.

So I scooted, searching through my head for a topic of conversation so you wouldn't stare at my hair and my brother's baseball T-shirt, which was a children's extra-large and at least fit me better than my own outgrown "women's small" shirts did. I was dressed in my best outfit that day—still, I could tell everyone was staring, including you, Lorelei.

"You know Morse code?" I finally asked, frantically. I knew it wasn't a perfect ice breaker, but I was feeling really stressed-out by then and my poor brain couldn't latch on to anything better. I'd been listening to a guy talk about Morse code on the car radio the night before, while I peeled carrots for the stew cooking over the campfire. I was in charge of dinner because my mother was at the campground ladies' rest room, washing out our underwear for school.

★　★　★

After a few minutes, when the Morse code conversation wasn't going anywhere, I switched topics. I brought something up that shocked me myself as I said it, because it was so personal. But I was desperate to say something normal and friendly and casual so you wouldn't think I was weird or something.

"I'm originally from the constellation Cassiopeia," I confided. Remember?

Well, actually that wasn't really confiding, because as you now know, I'm not from Cassiopeia, strictly speaking. But I am a star person, since the sky has been the roof over my head for so long. Since the stars are my best friends, and the sharers of my truest secrets. Only, well, I guess I'm sharing them with you now, right?

You just looked at me in surprise when I said that, I hoped because you were so impressed. Then the box you had your school supplies in slid from your lap

145

and crashed to the floor, and you turned a deep red, especially your neck.

"That was a weird thing to say," you told me.

I didn't know what else to talk about, after that. It looked like you were going to think I was weird no matter what I said. But I figured that was probably just because of Tyrone's T-shirt.

★   ★   ★

A couple minutes later the bell rang, and as everybody scrambled I realized with a panicky jolt that the secretary hadn't given me instructions beyond waiting in the gym! That's always been something I dread more than almost anything else—not knowing where to go in a new school.

I sort of got caught in the flow of bodies and swept along down what looked like the main hall of the building, and then I saw your hair up ahead and realized that you were a few yards in front of me. What a relief!

"You got math first period?" I kind of yelled to you, just guessing.

"No, history," you said. "Excuse me, I've got to hurry."

"I've got history, too," I lied, since I didn't know what in the world I was supposed to have. Well, history seemed as good as anything else. "I'll walk you."

★   ★   ★

When I sat in that empty seat next to yours in history, I took one look out that big bank of windows on my other side and the horrible suffocating panic I'd felt since entering the school dissolved. Oh, those mountains! Those beautiful, beautiful mountains, like escalators leading up to the stars. I could barely pull my eyes off them, but I knew the strict-looking teacher in there would yell at me if I didn't look like I was listening, at least a little. The last thing I needed was to draw attention to myself, when I probably wasn't supposed to be in his class to begin with. I took out a sheet of notebook paper and began working on constellation sketches, imagining how clear they'd look from the tops of those snow-covered peaks. I hoped it looked like I was taking notes.

I glanced across the aisle, read your name on your history notebook. Lori. Lori Sumner.

As I sketched I daydreamed about whispering across to you, asking if you'd go hiking with me, up the slope of one of those mountains. There was an impatient, tingly feeling in my legs from wanting to be on those mountains, touching the sky. And the thought of sharing that with a friend, a person who really knew you and liked you, was almost too good to imagine. If we could only, only stay here . . .

And then I glanced up, alerted by a sudden silence in the class, to see the teacher striding toward me. He glanced at my star doodling, grimaced, and slapped an enrollment card down on my desk.

And everything sort of came crashing in on me.

I looked miserably down at that glaring white form and could see written between its lines that I would never climb those mountains. I would never have friends here, maybe not even one fast friend like I tried to make just about everywhere we went. As I'd suspected somewhere deep inside me, Greenpoint was too good to be true. Only people with real addresses could have real friends, real dreams.

And I didn't have a real address, and hadn't for a long time.

It was never easy putting down all those "Elm Streets" on all those blank enrollment forms. But at least all those other times I'd pretty much accepted that we'd soon be moving on, and hadn't gotten my stupid hopes so far up. I could almost think of it as a game, those other times, and that made it easier. This time, though, writing those nine miserable letters would be horrible, because I cared. I didn't want to lie this time! I didn't want to risk being found out, humiliated in front of everybody in class! Besides, I was going on thirteen now—getting too old for all the fibbing and sneaking around.

The truth hit me full in the stomach as I stared at that card. I was sick of living out of the station wagon. Sick, sick to death of it.

I felt terribly guilty thinking that. And also, sort of free, finally getting that thought out of my heart and into the open of my mind.

When the bell rang, I ran back to the gym. There, I climbed high on the hanging rope. I swung from the rings for all I was worth. When my arms got tired or a class came in there, I went to the janitors' mop room in the corner and hid in the darkness for a while. Then when the coast was clear, I'd come back out and climb again.

I stayed there for a long time, all the rest of the day. I tried to connect to the sky, the only place I could call home.

Still, the old sky magic wasn't working very well. Maybe I was outgrowing it, like Tyrone's shirts.

And then, toward the end of the afternoon, I saw you come sneaking in, Lorelei. I saw you hiding behind the bleachers, watching me.

And I figured out from that that you did want to be my friend. And that only made me feel worse, because that's what I wanted, too, and yet I felt deep inside that we would be moving on and so it could never happen.

Chapter 23

When school was finally over that afternoon I was too miserable to ask Tyrone how his day had gone, but he told me anyway while we sat on the curb waiting for Daddy to pick us up.

"I've already got a best friend, Vern!" he said breathlessly. "His name's Russell and he's got a baseball autographed by Ozzie Smith and everything. And he gave me the crusty parts of his bologna sandwich."

"Mama told you not to eat other people's food," I told him listlessly. But I couldn't really blame him. We'd been short of supplies that morning, and had each just brought half an apple and part of the stew from last night, cold and greasy in a peanut butter jar.

"So you like it here?" I asked, wanting to keep hearing his voice so I wouldn't feel so empty inside. "You think it's okay?"

"It's great!" he answered. "People like me here. Miss Harmon said I'm like a celebration because I'm the new kid."

He probably meant like a celebrity, but I didn't have the energy to correct him.

"Yeah. That's how it is in fifth grade," I sighed. "You get attention when you're new, instead of just getting shoved around in the halls and laughed at."

"And then Miss Harmon asked me where I moved here from, and when I said Texas she said that was just great because they are studying the Alamo and cowboy stuff in social studies! And Russell said that Texas cowboys were the fastest guns in the West!"

I guess I was still thinking of you, Lorelei, and how I wished we could be real, forever friends. Because his words made my chest feel tighter, as something true and awful occurred to me. Over the past months, I'd become one of the fastest friends in the West. Maybe even *the* fastest friend. Bang, bang here today. Bang, bang gone tomorrow. Hello, and then good-bye—period. So what was the use of even trying?

And where was Daddy, anyway? The buses had been gone for nearly an hour. I kicked up a stir of dusty gravel, then wished I hadn't when I remembered the showers at our campground were turned off for the winter. Mom had said we'd wait for a couple of more days before going to the YMCA and asking to use their showers.

"I bet you didn't even have to fill out an enrollment card, did you?" I asked Tyrone.

He shook his head and shrugged, happily.

"They just liked me fine like I was without any old card," he explained.

By the time Daddy finally picked us up, it was nearly dark.

He was in a bad mood, too. I took it that he'd had no luck job hunting.

★　★　★

That night I sat by the embers of the campfire after everybody else was asleep, and stared across at the hulking shapes that were mountains, clothed in mysterious darkness.

It was cold. Very cold. I opened the door of the car as quietly as I could, and reached across the Tyrone lump in the He-Man sleeping bag for one of my own blankets.

I wrapped it around my shoulders like a shawl and walked into the darkness, to be more alone with the mountains and the stars that crowned them.

At the entrance to the campground there was a big map, which I'd memorized the day we'd arrived, showing the location and names of all the mountains. I knew the largest, the one that sort of loomed like a queen over the others, was called Hackberry Slope. I walked toward Hackberry Slope that night in the quiet darkness.

And it was then, when I was a few hundred yards from our campsite (there were no other campers anywhere around—probably too cold, being early winter) that it happened.

All of my "finder" instincts suddenly revved themselves up to a fever pitch, and every nerve in my body seemed to vibrate into life. My house—it was there, on that mountain! I'd never known anything with such absolute certainty in my life!

The Victorian house that my key opened—it was high up on Hackberry Slope! Waiting, beckoning.

In a flash, that changed everything. Just everything! All I would have to do now at school would be just give the usual "Elm Street" address on my enrollment card, knowing that would be very temporary. In a short time, when we'd found and settled into our house on Hackberry Slope, I could simply ask to change the card, and say we'd moved to our permanent home.

Our permanent home!

No more lying, no more sneaking around. I could do it one more time, could fake one more enrollment card. Because our house was here.

Just waiting! I could feel it, stronger than I'd ever felt anything in my life!

We were home, after all. I just knew it, in my bones.

★ ★ ★

I went quickly back to camp and drifted off to sleep so relieved that I dreamt all night I was floating happily through the clear, cold sky. And as I dressed in the freezing car the next morning, I suddenly realized I could take a shower at school after gym. And I also realized I could think of you now as a friend, Lorelei. After all, why couldn't I have a friend, like Tyrone did, since I knew now that we would find our house and be staying?

Everything was suddenly falling into perfect place.

At school I waited for you in our spot, underneath the bleachers.

I'd decided that to sort of kick off the true beginning of our friendship, I would explain about being a finder, which was my most private secret. So I told you, especially about finding the key and exactly what that meant to me, hoping you'd understand.

I couldn't really tell if you did or not.

In history class, I just couldn't wait a second longer to begin putting my house-discovering plans in motion.

"We could go climbing, up Hackberry Slope," I whispered across the aisle to you.

You didn't say anything, but that was probably because Mr. Parkins brought me another enrollment card at that moment. I was sure you would have been as enthused and excited as I was if you'd had time to answer.

Later, in phys. ed., you seemed surprised that I didn't want to show off climbing the rope. Why would I want to show off when you'd just bombed out on the rope yourself? Couldn't you see I wanted to be friends, and friends don't get their kicks from making their friends feel bad? I don't know, Lorelei, you seem to have kind of a hang-up about that, which I can't understand at all.

★　★　★

Back at the campground that night I tried to figure out whether or not I should tell you that we live in the back of a station wagon. I'd never told anyone from any of the schools I've gone to. I'd never had a reason to, since "Elm Street" had satisfied the teachers and I'd never wanted to invite any kids over.

But I did want to invite you over, Lorelei. I could see it all, in my head. First we'd hike up Hackberry Slope, and then eat hot dogs around the fire. I figured, big as the slope was, it might take us several afternoons to find the house. Several hot dog meals, some with marshmallows.

Still, maybe you'd be shocked, or even disgusted. About the station wagon. I just didn't know.

By the time I went to sleep I'd kind of decided to play it by ear, to just see what the next day brought.

★　★　★

It turned out to bring disaster.

To begin with, Daddy was on the warpath the second he woke up. He got mad when he couldn't find the matches for the morning fire, and threw all the blankets out of the car onto the ground. Tyrone's zebra Randy landed in a puddle, and Tyrone ran behind the car door and cried quietly.

After Daddy took off, driving fast and angry in the direction of the main highway, Mama washed the mud off Randy in the freezing water of the creek.

"What's wrong with him?" I asked her, and she knew I meant Daddy, not Tyrone or Randy.

"Same old thing," Mama whispered, her fingers blue from the creek water. "There just aren't jobs here, Vernita. Maybe in the tourist season, come summer. But . . . but November is about as far from summer as you can get."

My throat got tight with panic then, but I kept hanging onto the thought of our house, hidden in the mountains just waiting for us. I trusted my finder's instincts more than I trusted what Mama had just said. I grabbed my necklace, and looked up at the mountains, more determined than ever to get us out of this mess, to plant us here once and for all. Time. That was the problem. If I just had time.

"Don't worry, Mama," I said. "I kind of have a plan."

But she didn't seem to hear, just kept staring down at Randy, her fingers trembling as she wrung him dry.

★　★　★

School was a disaster, too. In the gym, I had to face the fact that you evidently didn't even want to be friends.

"It's not like we're official friends," you said, flat-out. "Just because you messed up on the rope for me."

I didn't know how to answer that. That's why I just walked away from you.

And then in history, everything came crashing down on my head. Mr. Parkins had checked things out and figured out I faked my address. It was the very thing I'd worried most about happening at every school I'd been to. But why did it have to happen here, of all places? He made a big deal of it, too, humiliated me in front of everybody, including you.

So I left history, too. I snuck into the gym again and began slowly climbing the rope. I pretended to be Cassiopeia, shining in the sky. But that doesn't work as well anymore as it did a few months ago, when I wasn't nearly thirteen.

When you're nearly thirteen you know pretty much exactly who you are, like it or not, know what I mean, Lorelei? There's not really that much hope of escape from your own self.

When I got to the top of the rope I huddled up there, tried to just fade into the rusty metal of the rafters. Tried to be at home there, above the world, like birds are.

And then, you showed up.

"You can tell me to leave if you want to be alone," you called up to me. "I've got your constellation paper. It's beautiful."

"You're going to be late for class," I called back down to you, my throat throbbing so I could hardly get the words out. The bell had just rung for second period to start.

"Yeah. I'm not going, though, so no big deal."

"Why not?"

"Because I want to tell you something."

I held my breath and closed my eyes tight.

You moved from where you'd been standing, directly below me, and went to sit on the floor and lean back against the bleachers. I slid a little way down the rope to listen better.

"It's just that . . . well, I don't think you should have to tell Mr. Parkins or anybody else your real address or phone or even your real name unless you want to. I mean, I actually go by a false name here at school myself."

Now that was a shock—I wasn't the only person faking their way through life!

"My real name is Lorelei, like the graceful, ancient sea siren who lured sailors to destruction with her enchanting beauty," you whispered.

I froze all over. It got mysteriously, eerily quiet. I realized then that was because I'd been tapping my teeth before.

"My real name is Vernita," I whispered back to you. I guess I hoped you'd realize from that how sacred and secret your true name would always be in my hands.

Then Miss Arklemyer came in, and I hurried back up the rope. She gave you that exercise manual, which really got you in a, no offense, rotten mood. When Miss Arklemyer went back out, I slid down the rope, but I was almost sorry I had when I saw how mad you were.

"This is just definitely all I need," you sort of snarled, looking like you were about to cry, and possibly hit me with the book. "As if my life wasn't a mess enough right now!"

I thought about that for a minute. Now, Lorelei, don't take this the wrong way, okay? But you are slightly loose and jiggly, sort of out of shape. And it seems like if you were a little toned up things might go easier for you, in rope-climbing and stuff. I figured Miss Arklemyer was right and an exercise plan was just what you needed, though I wouldn't have dared to say that to you, especially in the mood you were in.

And then, it was like a window threw itself open in my brain, sort of like it had the night I realized our house was on Hackberry Slope. I felt every finder instinct tingling, and realized the answers to both our problems were to be found right there under our noses!

"I could go home with you and sit on your feet while you do sit-ups and push-ups!" I suggested, so full of sudden hope I could hardly breathe. "And we could work on your endurance by climbing Hackberry Slope!"

You could get in shape. And I could find my house!

Chapter 24

We left school right then and there, to go to your house to get started on the whole thing. I could tell our plan was perfect, because there was even a fresh jet trail dividing the sky as we walked—a sign of luck if ever there was one.

But we didn't make it, as you know as well as I do.

My dad caught us, drove by as we were walking down the street having that wonderful discussion about gravity.

He was really mad—probably madder than I've ever seen him. A guy in a bar had just told him that he was a fool for coming to the Ozarks. The guy said the Ozarks only had work in the summer, and then at minimum wage. The guy said my dad should have his head examined for ever suspecting otherwise. And then the other guys in the bar chimed in and agreed with him about all of that.

So Daddy was on his way back to camp yesterday to

yell at Mama and then to make a new plan to go somewhere else when he saw us and grabbed me and took me back to camp with him.

★ ★ ★

Last night there were no stars. Did you notice? None.

Tyrone and I stayed by the campfire while Mama and Daddy talked till real late in the station wagon. Daddy's voice was loud part of the time. Once we heard him slam something around on the dashboard. It got colder and colder. I started worrying about Tyrone, who has sort of a cold anyway. He was sniffling and snorting, and wiping his nose every so often either on his sleeping bag or Randy.

"You okay?" I whispered to him. Though why I felt like we had to whisper I don't know. I just always feel like that on awful nights like last night.

And then I noticed something—Tyrone was wearing a Cardinals hat! It was pretty beat up, and part of the cardinal's head had chocolate or something melted on it. But it was a Cards hat, just the same.

"Ronie, your hat!" I whispered.

"Neat, huh?" He pulled down on the brim, grinning ear to ear. "Russell gave it to me to keep forever and ever. He's my friend."

I didn't want to cry, especially not in front of Ronie.

I hadn't cried since I said good-bye to the Arch that day when I was still eleven, and I kept thinking this was a weird time to start. When I was almost thirteen and everything.

But I'm not stupid, and I know that not many

things in life are certain. But a few sad things, at the moment, were.

One certain thing was that conversations like my parents were now having always ended up with us moving the next day.

And another certain thing was that our house was on Hackberry Slope, and would stay there forever now, unfound. So near, and yet because of time running out on me, so far.

And I knew Tyrone's T-shirts weren't going to fit me much longer. Then what would I wear, Daddy's T-shirts?

And I knew I had a friend here, too, a beginning friend, like Ronie did. But tomorrow my almost-friend would sit in the gym before first period and wonder where I'd gone.

So I cried, hard. And after a while, Ronie stretched his skinny arm around my shoulders, and handed me Randy for comfort.

Chapter 25

～ **I** didn't interrupt Vern once through her whole story, even when she expressed the opinion that I needed an exercise plan. I mean, what could I say? I was pretty stunned, to tell you the truth. I kept wondering how she could talk about her life like she did, like it was so normal and everything. It was easier for me to imagine living on Mars than living in the back of a car. At least on Mars you would have room for a clothes closet and could have a real kitchen, if you could get an oxygen supply rigged up.

Now that I knew what things were like for her, I felt totally differently about Vern. She didn't seem the least bit scuzzy or weird now. She actually seemed pretty smart and brave, as a matter of fact. A tough and hardy survivor, like you think of the early pioneers being, pushing through the desert out there in their covered wagons.

When she stopped talking, evidently finished with

her story, I took a deep breath and frowned at the sky, trying to take everything in. I suddenly noticed that it wasn't afternoon any longer. I heard a mourning dove, a sure sign of nearing sunset. Vern turned toward that sound, too, with a little shiver, and I got up out of the leaves and tried to shake the kinks out of my stiff body.

"Here," Vern said, quickly handing me her key.

"No," I pushed it back toward her, shocked. "It's yours, Vern. Somewhere there's a house for you that it opens."

She furrowed her eyebrows and shook her head. "No. See, Lorelei, you don't understand. This was my house, all right. It's just that everything that's found isn't meant to be kept. I knew the second I went inside that it was my house to find, not to keep."

She stood up, threw the hood of her sweatshirt over her greasy hair, and started leading us back down the mountain.

★   ★   ★

It was hard going down. Cold, and dark. I kept shivering, hoping I didn't lose sight of Vern's back in the twilight.

When we came around to the campground side of the mountain, Vern's family's fire looked like the beam from a lighthouse—the only point of light and warmth in all this wilderness spreading in all directions.

"Looks cozy," I said, forgetting for a second the awful pirate-father waiting there to snatch Vern and make her life miserable.

Vern stopped and stuck her hands into her pockets,

then stared down at that flickering fire and the tiny, shadowy shapes gathered around it.

"He only wants something better for us," she said quietly, like she was talking more to herself than to me. "We started out from St. Louis looking for that, and now we're going back to St. Louis still looking for it. Just something better, but it moves all the time just a little ahead of us."

She turned clear around to face me.

"Don't blame him, okay, Lorelei? Because everything he ever does he just does because he loves us."

My chest suddenly felt like someone was reaching inside and squeezing my heart.

"I won't see you again!" I said, that knowledge the thing that was putting the squeeze on me. "Ever."

She turned partway back around, so I couldn't see her face very well in the darkness.

"Maybe not," she said. "But maybe. Maybe I'll come back when I'm grown and on my own. Maybe I'll fix up the house. Will you check on it for me sometimes?"

"Sure," I said, then swallowed. "Uh, Vern? Up there on the mountain, when you asked what I was saying this morning? Well, I was saying that if I didn't find you today, then I was not meant to ever have you for a friend. But I did find you. And I'm real glad about that, okay?"

I could feel her smiling in the darkness.

"Yeah, Lorelei. Okay. Me, too."

Chapter 26

At the foot of the mountain I left her.

At sea level, we left each other.

A sky creature, a sea creature. We said good-bye quickly and she went toward her campfire. I ran most of the way home.

Sure enough, when I got to my own bathroom I weighed myself, and I'd lost two pounds.

★　★　★

That night, I put a chair under my bedroom doorknob for privacy and scraped the black paint from one of my bedroom windows. I hung Vern's key there. Then I fell into bed, exhausted, and looked at the sky through that one square of window. For a long time I watched the stars behind the key, outlining it.

I finally really understood, then, what Vern had meant the day she told me the sky was like a big roof over everything, so in a way you were at home everywhere. She was my friend, and always would be, no matter where she was. The same sky would be over us both. I went to sleep thinking that.

I woke with a jolt just at dawn, and knew in my bones Vern was leaving. I could feel the damp cold in that station wagon, could picture in my mind the way the gray morning sky would look moving outside Vern's cracked back window.

I felt her lying there, one hand under her head, as the mountains raced away and the hills of Missouri took their place.

★　★　★

I was pretty sure Mom and Dad knew I'd missed a little school lately, but neither of them said anything about it. They just kept looking me over during breakfast, trying to act like they weren't worried. Dad hid behind the paper, but left it sagging on my side so he could explore me out the sides of his glasses. Mom stayed puttering near the stove where she could take everything in.

"No pancakes for me, thanks, Mom," I said, reaching for a banana. "I'm trying to lose a little weight."

She opened her mouth, and I thought she looked a little pale, but she evidently thought I was sick or something, not just unhungry. So she let it go.

When I got up to leave the room, I was so sore I could hardly limp. But the pain felt good in a way. Like a start, a change for the better. If I checked on Vern's house up Hackberry Slope three or four times a week, pretty soon I'd be as skinny as Louise, practically.

It was hard sitting alone in the gym that first morning. Harder than it had even been before Vern. Hard in a different way. I didn't feel self-conscious now, as much as just plain sad. I tried not to think of her swinging her long scabby-kneed leg there beside me. I couldn't believe I missed the clicking of that stupid key against her teeth, but I did.

There in the gym, where she'd practically flown through the sky on ropes and rings when no one was watching, she seemed to be everywhere.

In history, Louise turned back to glance at me several times during the hour.

"You okay?" she mouthed in my direction once.

Cheryl saw her and turned around to frown in my direction, then to stare at Louise like she was crazy for talking to me. But Louise didn't look embarrassed. In fact, she just gave Cheryl a "none of your business" stare right back, until Cheryl shrugged and dropped her eyes back to her book.

★　★　★

That night I wrote Vern a letter.

I got it all the way written before I remembered I had no idea what her address in St. Louis was. I wadded up the paper, and looked at her key, hanging silver in my window.

The next morning was Saturday, and I forced myself to ride my poor old rusted up bike around the block a couple of times. My legs were still killing me from mountain climbing, but I figured all that pain of the past two days would be wasted if I didn't go on with it.

No pain no gain, as the jocks say.

It was after that bike ride, when I was sweaty and tired and hungry for something I was going to try hard to resist eating, that I went in my room and knew it was time for a change.

I took down the octopus first.

I held him out in front of me, waved his longest tentacle with one hand and waved back to him with the other.

"Bye, bye," I said, then laughed. I crumpled him up and stuffed him into the trash sack. I ripped off all the other paper fish then and trashed them, too.

The room looked really hideous with everything black and wads of tape all over the empty walls. The floor was scuffed by then from walking on that paint with shoes on, too. Everything was really a mess.

I sank to the floor, and Louise swam over to mouth around on the edge of the tank and visit.

"What do you think, girl? Feel like some sunshine in here?" I asked.

Chapter 27

If you think painting a pink room black is hard, you should try painting a black room yellow. It took me every spare second of a whole week to get on enough coats of yellow to cover the walls. And then I started sanding the floor, and that was no picnic, either. The windows were pretty easy. The paint came off with a putty knife without too much hassle.

My mother was so happy about my room she didn't even try too hard to shove food down me, like I'd been afraid she would. In fact, she didn't even stop me the three afternoons I went out to check on Vern's house.

I didn't make it all the way up the mountain to the house any of those first times. I was too sore, and it was hard going, alone. But I made it a little farther each day.

By the time Vern had been gone about two weeks, I

had gotten a system together where I dressed in my jogging suit right after school on Monday, Wednesday, and Friday and went to Hackberry Slope right after class.

It was on Friday of that second week that Louise came into the gym when I was just tying my shoes, and asked if she could go along.

"Why?" I asked, flustered and confused. "I mean, aren't you busy? With your friends?"

She sat down on the bench between the rows of lockers and started picking at one fingernail.

"Well, you know, Lori. I'm just not sure about them. I mean, I told you I never have been able to talk to anybody like we used to talk together."

She looked up then, and her eyes were shiny.

"I used to think being accepted by the popular crowd would be just about perfect, just heaven, you know, Lor? Remember when we were chubby little kids, and we used to think they were all so neat and cool and everything? But if you can't be yourself . . . if you can't really talk to the people you're with . . . oh, Lori, I don't know. I just feel so alone all the time now."

I opened my locker and threw my spare sweatshirt toward her.

"Okay then, suit up. But don't smell it under the armpits," I cautioned.

She smiled, and then laughed, and then we laughed together, just like old times.

★　★　★

Well, not exactly like old times.

Louise dropped me once, and though she's started

171

sitting with me again sometimes in the gym in the morning, she still talks to the popular kids a lot.

But I've got some other friends myself now. This may sound a little strange, but I met them in the salad bar line in the cafeteria. Yeah, there are several other people at Greenpoint trying to lose weight, and we sit together in the cafeteria, out of the line of temptation, nowhere within smelling distance of the spaghetti and chicken and stuff. We're sort of like a little support group for each other. I really like Ellen and Tracy especially—they're in a couple of my classes. We're sort of birds of a feather, I guess.

Birds of a feather—ha! Vern would appreciate that one.

I still hate that gym rope, but I can climb it now, almost halfway to the top. Partly because my weight's coming down, partly because my muscle tone is improving. I owe that to Vern, who almost was my trainer in person, and then sort of was anyway, even after she'd gone.

Seven weeks after she left, I got a postcard from her. Only one. And she forgot to put her return address on it, so I couldn't write back.

"Dear Lorelei," it said. "We have our old trailer back, and I wish you could see my bear rug. Keep my key safe, okay? Your friend, Vernita Hittlinger. P.S. I've retired from being the fastest friend in the West—ha! ha!"

All I could do with that postcard was read between the lines.

She'd called me Lorelei—the only person to ever

172

do so. If I could see her or write to her, I would tell her I'm a land animal again now, called Lori.

Her bear rug? Oh yeah—Herman.

Keep my key safe. Yes, I will. Always.

It embarrasses me now to remember how I almost made fun of Vern's skeleton key when she first showed it to me. I thought it was useless, but now I see it just had to be in the right hands, hands that believed in it. I hope some of Vern's finder ability rubbed off on me. I think maybe it did, or maybe it's starting to now that I've got her key hanging in my window all the time. I found that perfect yellow paint for my room. And when I moved my bed to sand the floor under it, I found a hairbrush I'd been missing. And, of course, I've found Ellen and Tracy.

The way she signed the card meant something, too—Vernita Hittlinger. The name of a girl, a person, a true somebody in the world.

But it was that P.S. that made me feel really good and hopeful about her. It meant she'd abandoned her old system of making one friend fast. It meant that she was finally home.

Maybe, when Vern's grown and on her own, she'll actually make it back here, to our mountains. Maybe she'll even fix that old place up and live there, close to the sky. Stranger things have happened.

Or maybe it's enough for her to just know it's here, to just have "found" it.

I'm glad she called me "your friend" on the card. I guess I was her last fast friend—fast as in quick, and in our case, fast as in lasting. I'm glad I climbed Hackberry Slope with her, achey legs and all.

I miss her. But I feel good about her.

The picture on that postcard was of the Gateway Arch. A steel rainbow against a bright midwestern sky. I could easily imagine Vern standing happily there under it, a person in love with the sky but planted on firm ground, at last.

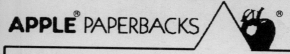

APPLE® PAPERBACKS

Pick an Apple and Polish Off Some Great Reading!

BEST-SELLING APPLE TITLES

- ❏ MT43944-8 **Afternoon of the Elves** Janet Taylor Lisle — $2.75
- ❏ MT43109-9 **Boys Are Yucko** Anna Grossnickle Hines — $2.75
- ❏ MT43473-X **The Broccoli Tapes** Jan Slepian — $2.95
- ❏ MT42709-1 **Christina's Ghost** Betty Ren Wright — $2.75
- ❏ MT43461-6 **The Dollhouse Murders** Betty Ren Wright — $2.75
- ❏ MT43444-6 **Ghosts Beneath Our Feet** Betty Ren Wright — $2.75
- ❏ MT44351-8 **Help! I'm a Prisoner in the Library** Eth Clifford — $2.75
- ❏ MT44567-7 **Leah's Song** Eth Clifford — $2.75
- ❏ MT43618-X **Me and Katie (The Pest)** Ann M. Martin — $2.75
- ❏ MT41529-8 **My Sister, The Creep** Candice F. Ransom — $2.75
- ❏ MT42883-7 **Sixth Grade Can Really Kill You** Barthe DeClements — $2.75
- ❏ MT40409-1 **Sixth Grade Secrets** Louis Sachar — $2.75
- ❏ MT42882-9 **Sixth Grade Sleepover** Eve Bunting — $2.75
- ❏ MT41732-0 **Too Many Murphys** Colleen O'Shaughnessy McKenna — $2.75

Available wherever you buy books, or use this order form.

Scholastic Inc., P.O. Box 7502, 2931 East McCarty Street, Jefferson City, MO 65102

Please send me the books I have checked above. I am enclosing $_____ (please add $2.00 to cover shipping and handling). Send check or money order — no cash or C.O.D.s please.

Name _____

Address _____

City_____ State/Zip _____

Please allow four to six weeks for delivery. Offer good in the U.S.A. only. Sorry, mail orders are not available to residents of Canada. Prices subject to change.

APP591